Sweet Revenge

A Standalone Novella

Samantha Cole

Suspenseful Seduction Publishing

Her high school bully is the last person Allondra Dawson wants to see.

Once, she loved handsome, infuriating Weston Lockhart—until he tried to humiliate her in front of their entire sophomore class.

Years later, when Allie runs into West, he doesn't recognize her.

It's the perfect opportunity for revenge . . .

She'll make him crave her, then walk away and shatter him.

But teasing and flirting become seduction, and the pleasure is too delicious to stop.

Too late, she realizes she's falling for him again.

Will he break her heart a second time when he learns why she schemed her way into his bed?

Chapter 1

Allondra Dawson tried to focus on what her chemistry teacher, Mr. Patel, was saying to the class, but her brain kept diverting to the boy sitting beside her. Weston Lockhart—aka the cutest guy in the whole school, the second-string quarterback and only sophomore on the varsity football team, and Allondra's crush.

Sigh.

She'd been in love with him for over a year but only dared to talk to him during her tutoring sessions or unless he said something to her first. While she was a straight-A student, math and science were her favorite subjects that she excelled in. After acing the first two exams earlier in the year, Mr. Patel had asked if she'd be willing to tutor other students. Initially, she'd been hesitant, but when West, standing nearby, said he could use the extra help, Allondra immediately accepted the position.

Chemistry and world history were the only two classes they had in common. For the latter, though, the students sat alphabetically, so West's desk was one row over and toward the back of the room while hers was in the front. It was hardly a vantage point for her to ogle him subtly. But during chemistry, he sat right beside her. She was almost always the first person in the room—a good three to four minutes before the bell rang since her English class was only a few classrooms down the hall. She eagerly awaited West's arrival each day. As she'd settled into her desk, pulling out her notebook, textbook, and pen, her gaze would dart toward the door whenever someone entered. When he finally strode into class—tall, dark, handsome, and confident, with a boisterous laugh, adorable dimples, and charming personality—Allondra's heart pounded, and her mouth watered.

Even though they were the same age, West could easily pass for a junior or senior. Meanwhile, Allondra looked like she was still a freshman or younger despite going through puberty at the age of twelve. Despite her baby fat, her bra size was only an A-cup, and she hadn't gained much height yet. Her father was over six feet tall while her mother was five feet eight, so it stood to reason she would eventually add to her five-foot-two frame.

She'd had a few pre-teen and teenage crushes, but those had been on celebrities she undoubtedly would never meet. With West, he sat three feet away from her, and if brave enough, she could reach over and touch his muscular bicep.

But she wasn't brave enough. She suspected she never would be. What would it be like, though, to be West's girlfriend? To be popular and go on dates with him? To eventually marry him someday?

Sigh.

A girl could dream, right?

The bell rang, jolting Allondra from her useless fantasy over something that would never happen. She knocked her book off the desk, and it landed with a heavy thud on the ugly tiled floor as everyone else got to their feet. Before she could bend over to retrieve it, West picked up the textbook and handed it to her with a smile and a wink. "Good thing it didn't land on your foot. You could've broken a few toes with that."

A nervous titter escaped her as butterflies took flight in her stomach. "Y-yeah. Thanks."

It appeared he was about to say something more, but then a cheerleader, Tessa Jameson, grabbed him by the arm. She gave Allondra the evil eye and a sneer before pasting on a brilliant smile for the usual target of her flirtation. "C'mon, West. Walk me to my next class. I want to tell you about the party at my house on Saturday." Her tone made it obvious Allondra wouldn't be invited—not that she expected to be.

"Uh . . . sure." Grabbing his books, West glanced at Allondra. "See you later in the library?" That's where they held their tutoring sessions.

Her head bobbled as her gaze dropped to the floor, and her cheeks burned. "Um, yeah. Of course."

"C'mon, West. Let's go." Tessa tugged on his arm, and then, moments later, they walked out the door together.

Sigh.

Gathering up her things, Allondra got ready for her next destination. She wasn't in a rush since it was her study hall period in one of the lunchrooms, where she would sit alone and do her math homework. Even if the monitors let the students talk in low voices about anything other than schoolwork, Allondra wouldn't be engaging with anyone. She didn't belong to any of the cliques assigned to that room—hell, she was barely friends with anyone in her entire class. There were a few other wallflowers that she hung out with—they were all in the school band—but that was about it. No BFF or someone she could share her secrets and dreams with. At least she could discuss those things with her cousin, who attended another high school about twenty minutes away, where she was an all-star volleyball player with many friends. Despite their differences, the two girls had been close all their lives. Allondra would give anything to be in the same school district as Sadie. As her Aunt Emily would say, they were thick as thieves when they got together.

Shyness had plagued Allondra since first grade after two girls had bullied her during recess, tripping her and making her fall flat on her face and break her glasses. All the other students had just laughed, and the embarrassment still haunted her years later. Since then, she'd tried to avoid being a target for further bullying by minding her own business and staying off the mean girls' radar as much as possible.

Instead of a popular cheerleader as she'd dreamed of being while attending elementary school, she hadn't been coordinated enough to do a simple cartwheel and, instead, had ended up as a piccolo player in the marching band. One student among a sea of others in matching purple and gold polyester uniforms that were hot and itchy as hell.

After quickly stopping at her locker to switch out several textbooks in her book bag, she headed toward the lunchroom and entered the girls' restroom across the hall just as two juniors walked out, giggling and chatting like best friends. A little jealous and annoyed at their perkiness, Allondra rolled her eyes and then found herself alone in the bathroom. She approached one of the sinks and stared at her reflection in the mirror above it.

Between her short stature, flat chest, and baby fat, there was no way anyone would be captivated by her. She craved a body that would make boys—especially West—stand up and take notice. Even if she had feminine curves in all the right places, like Tessa and the other cheerleaders, there were her eyeglasses and braces to contend with. At least she'd somehow avoided being plagued by acne. However, with mud-brown hair that loved to frizz in the humidity and boring hazel eyes, Allondra couldn't attract a teenage boy if she stripped down naked and proclaimed she was a slut to the entire school. Yeah, that was so not happening.

She would love to go out on a date with West or even one of the other cute boys in her class and experience love and her first kiss before going to college. As it were, she'd probably still be a virgin well into her twenties.

The Sophomore Social, an annual dance at Holden High, similar to the junior and senior proms but not as fancy, would take place in a few weeks, and Allondra already knew she wouldn't be attending. None of her male classmates would ask her to go with them, and there was no way she would go to the event alone. A few of her single bandmates were going together as a small group, but she didn't want to watch West dancing with whichever cheerleader or popular girl he invited to be his date. Probably Tessa. *Gag!*

She glanced at the pretty, antique watch her aunt had given her for her last birthday—two minutes left before the next bell rang. She'd get a demerit if she weren't in study hall before then. Too many demerits would result in detention—something she'd never gotten. Allondra was one of the "goody-two-shoes" girls, but there were days she wished she wasn't. She would love to be one of the popular girls, but that would probably mean she'd have to be a bully. It seemed like all the in-crowd were—except West. He was always nice to her. Then again, as far as she could tell, he was nice to everyone.

Entering one of the stalls, she locked the door behind her and set her book bag on a fold-down shelf to keep it off the floor. She then took one of the paper seat protectors from a dispenser and laid it in place. Excelling in biology and chemistry, she was very aware of what germs could be found in public restrooms. Pushing down her jeans, she squatted until she was only an inch or two from the seat. She wasn't risking sitting on it, even with the protective paper between her skin and the cold porcelain.

Once she was done relieving herself, she used a

few squares of toilet paper to clean herself, tossed the wad into the bowl, and stood. As she pulled up her pants, the door to the hallway swung open with a bang, and three girls burst in, laughing and talking loudly.

"I told you he's a dork!"

"Oh, I totally agree with you!"

"Can you believe he actually thought I'd go to the Sophomore Social with him? As if! I mean, come on. Seriously? I wouldn't be caught dead dating a loser like him."

Great. Allondra recognized their voices. Stacey St. James, Ashley Cromwell, and Madison Ford—cheerleaders, Tessa's BFFs, and Allondra's occasional tormentors if she got on their radar. Since that was the last thing she wanted right then, she slowly and silently pulled up the zipper of her jeans and waited for the trio to leave, hoping they wouldn't notice her feet under the stall door. They were in the same study hall as her but sat on the opposite side of the room near the baseball players so they could flirt shamelessly when the monitors weren't looking. Since demerits affected their status on the cheerleading squad, they couldn't be late for classes. If they were on time for the study period, Allondra probably would be, too, since crossing the hall and entering the lunchroom only took three seconds.

"Oh em gee! Speaking of dorks—did you hear who West is asking to the dance?"

Allondra stiffened at the mention of her crush. She really didn't want to know who he was taking, especially if it was the stuck-up Tessa. Maybe if she covered her ears, she wouldn't hear who it was.

Okay, stop acting like a kindergartener, you twit. Grow up!

"Who?"

"You'll never guess! Not in a million years!"

"Who, Stacey? Come on! Dish, girl!"

"Are you ready for this?" There was a long, dramatic pause, and then, "Allondra fuckin' Dawson! Can you believe that shit?"

Squeals of disbelief echoed off the tiled walls. Allondra's eyes widened, and she slapped her hand over her mouth to keep quiet. She had to have misheard but couldn't think of any other girl in their class with a similar-sounding name. There was no way West was asking her to the dance. Right? Not when he could invite Tessa or any of the other girls who hung all over him.

Oh, my God! Is he really going to ask me?

A split second of excitement about her dream come true was interrupted by, "What? Why the hell would he ask that nobody?"

The insult stung.

"Ryan told me West is doing it as a joke. He's going to ask her and then stand her up."

The girls cackled loudly as Allondra's eyes burned with hot tears.

"Oh, that's fucking awesome! I hope he does it somewhere we can video it."

"Yes! Oh, my God! That would be perfect!"

A joke. He's doing it as a joke.

Her body trembled, and she almost sat down hard on the toilet, stopping herself just in time. She couldn't let them know she was there. Not now. Not ever.

How could West do that to her? And in front of the whole school! She'd be mortified.

The three girls continued to babble for a few more moments, but Allondra only caught bits and pieces over the roar in her ears. Her chin quivered as she fought to remain silent and hold back the sobs that wanted to erupt from her throat. Of all the people who might pull a mean prank on her, she would have never imagined West being the one to do it. But Ryan Hayes was West's best friend. If anyone knew who he would invite and why, it would be Ryan. Her heart crumbled.

"C'mon," Stacey said. "Let's go. If I get another demerit, I'll miss tomorrow's game."

Chapter 2

The outside restroom door opened and closed again, with the threesome's voices fading as they crossed the hall. When silence finally surrounded her, Allondra's weakened knees gave out. She nearly fell into the toilet but caught herself in time, grabbing onto the nearby shelf and, in the process, knocking her book bag to the floor. She didn't care about getting dirt and germs on her bag since it wasn't as bad as having a piss-wet ass from the unflushed toilet.

The period bell clanged over the PA system, announcing that all students must be in their assigned classrooms, but she ignored it. She wasn't going into study hall after what she'd just heard. She'd rather earn her first demerit ever than sit in the lunchroom, knowing Stacey, Ashley, and Madison were most likely telling everyone what West's plans were. They'd stare and laugh at her from across the room, and she would squirm under their scrutiny, unable to escape for forty-five minutes when the bell rang again.

A heavy, dull ache took up residence in her body, and a wave of nausea roiled in her stomach, drowning the earlier butterflies. Trying to keep her sobs as low as possible in case someone entered the restroom, she leaned against the wall as tears scalded her cheeks before dripping onto the floor. This was the worst day of her young life. West's smiling face bounced around her mind as it often did, but she nearly vomited at the image this time.

How could she have been so wrong about him? Why was he scheming to play such a cruel joke on her? What had she ever done to him to deserve that? She tutored him all year to ensure he passed chemistry and never asked for anything in return. Yet, making her a laughingstock in front of the entire school was his way of thanking her? Fuck that!

Boys sucked. Most likely, men did too—her father and uncles being the exceptions. Her dad was the greatest man she knew, and she doubted there was another like him in her future. Someone who would treat her as if she were the most precious woman on earth. Allondra had hoped that West would be that man someday, but that dream had just been shattered. Her destiny was probably to be a crazy cat lady who lived alone and died a virgin at a ripe old age. Wonderful.

Long minutes passed before her tears and sobs ebbed. She used toilet paper to blow her nose and wipe her eyes. Shock and hurt slowly morphed into anger. Now that she had a heads-up about what West planned to do, she could shore up her defenses and come up with a response for when he asked her to the dance. Hopefully, he wouldn't do it today. The pain was too fresh, and she'd probably burst into tears again when she saw him next.

How could she avoid him? Despite only having two classes together, they often passed each other in the hallway between periods. And then there was the tutoring session that afternoon. The only thing that came to mind was going to the health office and feigning a headache, stomachache, or heart attack. Something, anything that would convince the nurse to let her go home. That would be another first. She hadn't gone to the health office for any reason other than dropping off paperwork for her annual physicals since elementary school. Since she was rarely sick, other than seasonal allergies, her parents wouldn't think she was faking it. Her mom wasn't working today, so she could easily come and pick Allondra up. That would work for now, but she couldn't stay home for the rest of the school year. She needed to talk to Sadie—her cousin would know what to do.

Gathering her things, she exited the stall and stared at her reflection in the mirror again, taking a shuddering breath to stave off another round of tears and blubbering. Her eyes were red and swollen, and her cheeks were pale, so at least she looked sick. With any luck, that would help convince the nurse to let her call her mother.

She quickly washed her hands and then splashed some water on her face before grabbing a few paper towels. While she wanted to appear ill for the nurse, she didn't want anyone else to see her looking like that. It would just give the bullies another reason to taunt and laugh at her. Glancing at her watch, she was surprised to see only seven minutes left until the end of the period. With any luck, she could get to the health office without running into anyone.

Opening the door, she hesitantly peeked out. The hallway was empty except for one student running in the opposite direction from her before sliding to a stop in front of a classroom and entering it. Keeping her head down, Allondra stepped out of the restroom and headed for the health office, misery growing inside her with every step. Those girls were right—she was a nobody and probably would always be.

Five days later . . .

ALLONDRA TAPPED HER PEN AGAINST HER THIGH, waiting for the bell to ring so she could get out of World History without giving into the urge to look over her shoulder at West sitting in the back of the room. She'd managed to avoid him since she'd heard about his plan to ask her out. At the health office the other day, she used agonizing menstrual cramps as her need to go home—she was in the middle of her period, so it'd been an ideal excuse. Her mother wouldn't question it since she'd had bad cramps a few times before. Thankfully, the nurse had taken pity on her and allowed Allondra to go home since she did look like she was in a lot of pain. If only it hadn't been from a broken heart. The only downfall was her mother had made an appointment with their gynecologist tomorrow for an examination.

It had been a rough few days for Allondra—first, the mess with West and then finding out her father's company was transferring him, and they were all moving to Denver after the end of the school year.

While she couldn't care less about going to a new school, she hated the thought of being three-quarters of the way across the country from the rest of their extended family—especially Sadie and Aunt Emily.

After her father broke the news the other night, her aunt invited the two girls for a sleepover to create as many memories as they could in the short time they had before Allondra's family moved. The two girls often spent weekend overnights at Aunt Emily's house, complete with pizza, movies, dancing, gossiping, and painting each other's nails.

Once her aunt had gone to bed, Allondra confessed to Sadie what West planned to do, and her cousin's response, after threatening to kick his ass, had been simple. "When he asks, just raise your chin, look bored, and tell him 'No, thanks.'"

They'd even practiced it a few times, with Sadie being West. Allondra still wasn't sure she could pull it off, but she really didn't have any better ideas.

She'd gotten out of tutoring for the rest of the year after using the upcoming move as an excuse that she no longer had time to stay after school to help the group. Mr. Patel was very understanding and asked the backup tutor to fill in for the remaining few weeks. With that taken care of, the only time Allondra hadn't been able to avoid West was when they had two classes together. History was easier since he sat far away from her, but chemistry had been excruciating, trying not to glance at him or burst into tears. Whenever he asked a question or tried to engage her in conversation, she'd kept her answers short or pretended not to hear him. Unfortunately, it hadn't seemed to deter him one bit.

Yesterday, he stood with a few sophomores, including his friend Ryan, a short distance from her locker. She hadn't heard what they were saying but noticed West glancing in her direction. Ryan followed his gaze and then said something that had everyone in the small group laughing, including West. Allondra's cheeks had burned, and tears threatened to fall as she slammed her locker shut and spun away. She then took the long way to her next class to avoid walking past them.

Only four weeks to go before the last day of school. After that, she would never have to see West or any of the mean in-crowd again. She was torn between wanting time to fly and hoping it would slow down so she could have more sleepovers at Aunt Emily's with Sadie.

When the bell rang, Allondra threw her books and pen into her bag and made a beeline for the door, managing to be the first one out of the room. She breathed a sigh of relief that she evaded the jerk again. Hurrying to her locker, she quickly spun the dial to unlock it and opened the door.

"Hey, Allondra."

She froze at the sound of West's voice. It seemed to have gotten deeper over the past year with each passing week, and despite not wanting it to, the delicious timbre sent shivers down her spine.

After a quick glance in his direction, she focused on searching for her math book. She kept her tone flat and her response short. "Hey."

He leaned casually against the row of lockers next to hers, holding his history textbook and a spiral notebook against his chest. Allondra did her best to control her breathing and blink back a few tears that wanted to well up.

"Are you okay? You're not tutoring the group anymore."

"I'm fine. I just have too much work of my own to do." It took everything in her not to look at him again. Maybe if she were rude, he'd go away.

"Listen, I wanted to ask you something."

Shit. Here it comes. You can do this. Just like you and Sadie practiced. "Yeah? What?"

She found her math book, stuck it into the bag, and put her history and Spanish books into the locker. West hesitated, probably wondering why she wasn't giving him her full attention.

"Um . . . I was wondering . . . uh . . . would you . . .

um . . . would you like to go to the Sophomore Social with me?"

Allondra swallowed hard and bit her lip. Her heart sank. Until he said those words, she'd prayed it had been a false rumor, but now she knew it was true. She couldn't stop herself from glancing around the hallway. What she saw had her stomach roiling and her knees quivering. While freshmen and some juniors strode down the hallway, chatting and seemingly oblivious to the drama unfolding, clusters of students from the sophomore class watched her and West with rapt interest. Some whispered to each other while others eagerly awaited her response. Several pointed their phones at her and West, clearly recording them while waiting for the big joke to be revealed and for the shy wallflower to be humiliated. Whatever happened in the next few seconds would be the talk of the tenth grade for days, if not weeks.

Her cheeks flushed, but somehow, she found the courage to tilt her chin up. She used a bored tone as Sadie had instructed. "No, thanks."

She caught a flash of shock in his eyes before she diverted her gaze, slammed her locker shut, then turned away and hurried through the mass of students toward her next class. Behind her, gasps, murmurs, and a few curses of disbelief reached her ears, but she ignored all of them. A lump formed in her throat, and she swiped her eyes, preventing several threatening tears from falling. Her emotions were split between anguish, contempt, and triumph. She was proud she hadn't given West and the rest of the in-crowd the satisfaction of humiliating her. Now, she'd be okay if she could only get through the last few weeks of school without falling apart.

Chapter 3

Twenty years later . . .

"ALLIE, WERE WE REALLY THAT DORKY BACK then?"

Allie grimaced as she eyed the five-by-eight photograph her cousin Sadie McKenna held. The framed image was from nearly two decades ago and had been sitting on an end table next to a sofa, which was nearly as old but still in fairly good condition. Both fifteen-year-old girls were grinning, each with an arm over the other's shoulder. While Sadie had the appearance of the cool, popular, athletic, and attractive teenager she'd been back then, Allie had been a nerdy wallflower. The photo had been taken at the end of her sophomore year at Holden High School, two weeks before she and her parents had moved to Denver.

At the time, while she'd known she would miss her Aunt Emily, Sadie, and the rest of her relatives in the area, Allie had looked forward to starting over in a new school and making friends. Anything would've been better than her time at HHS, being targeted by the mean girls and seeing that bastard West all the time. God, she hated the memories of those days.

Crestwood High School had been better than she'd hoped for. The rest of the summer had gone quickly with all the unpacking and decorating she and her parents had done at their new house. It'd taken a few weeks to settle into the new school and find a clique she fit into, but through it all, even with thousands of miles separating them, her cousin had been there for her. They'd often texted, Facetimed, and called, celebrating, commiserating, and supporting each other through different life events. That was why Sadie was now helping Allie sort through her deceased aunt's possessions.

Emily Thurman had been her father's sister, while Sadie was related to Allie on her mother's side, but the older woman had treated them both with the same amount of love as they grew up. She'd been widowed at a young age and never remarried or had any children of her own, but everyone close to Emily had been family to her, whether they were blood-related or not. Sadie had cried as hard as Allie when she'd heard the elderly woman had passed away two months ago. With Allie being the closest heir, most of the estate had been left to her upon Emily's death. The rest had been bequeathed to several charities.

"I was a dork. You belonged in *Teen Magazine*."

Sadie rolled her eyes. "You were *not* a dork—just a late bloomer. I mean, look at you now—you're fucking gorgeous. Hell, most of the people at Aunt Em's wake and funeral, who weren't family, had no clue who you were."

It was true. During the months following the move to Denver, Allie had shot up and out, adding five inches to her height and two cup sizes to her breasts. Her baby fat had finally shifted to where it enhanced her figure. Suddenly, she had cleavage, a narrower waist, and curvy hips. In other words, she'd become voluptuous. The chubbiness had left her face, showing off cheekbones and smooth, nearly flawless skin that more than one of her friends had said they'd kill for over the years. The braces had come off, and her parents allowed her to ditch the glasses at sixteen and arranged for her to get contacts. And now, she didn't even need those since having LASIK surgery a few years ago.

All of those changes had contributed to her gaining self-confidence, especially when the boys started to notice and flirt with her, but she'd still been a bit introverted for the rest of her high school years. While she'd made more friends in Colorado than in New York, it hadn't been until she attended college that her personality had truly emerged. Thankfully, her sorority sisters and a few mentors had helped draw her out of her shell. After she'd pledged to Chi Omega at Ridgeland University, she'd blossomed.

During her third year of college, a friend had convinced Allie to dye her hair a rich auburn with beautiful highlights, adding to her transformation from blah Allondra to chic Allie. Her mother and Sadie said the coloring lit up her face, and she loved it enough to keep it that way ever since. She was a completely different woman than the teenager she'd been, and sometimes, it seemed like her younger self had existed in another dimension. One she never wanted to visit again.

During Aunt Emily's wake, many people she'd known had asked who she was since she'd been standing in a receiving line with the family. Once she said her name, most had gaped momentarily before regaining their composure and offering her their condolences for her loss. It would've been comical if it hadn't been such a solemn occasion.

Bringing her attention back to the task at hand, Allie glanced around the living room. She still had so much to do and no idea where to begin. Thank goodness Sadie was more organized when it came to household stuff. Allie's office was tidy and efficient. Her apartment? Not so much.

Sadie handed her a piece of paper. "Okay, here's your list. Call the charity to pick up the pieces of furniture that are still in good condition, but you don't want to keep. Then arrange for a dumpster to be delivered by Friday. I put the name and number of the company that Pete's friend owns. Don't forget to tell Rich you're related to us—he'll give you a good deal. Then, grab everything on the shopping list while running your other errands. Pete and I will be here with the kids first thing on Saturday morning to help go through all the cabinets, drawers, closets, basement, and the garage."

Allie took the list from her cousin, mentally adding a few other chores to it. A stack of death certificates in her aunt's name had to be mailed to creditors, her health insurance carrier, the Social Security Agency administration, and the Department of Motor Vehicles. Emily's life insurer had already been notified since that money had been used for the funeral, with the remaining amount mailed to Allie in the form of a check. Other death certificates needed to be delivered to the utility companies, the town's tax office, Aunt Emily's bank, her financial planner, and her insurance agent for the house and the car still sitting in the driveway. Selling the five-year-old Buick was one more thing on an extensive checklist of things Allie had to do.

"Are you any closer to making a decision about whether to sell the house or move back here?" Sadie asked.

She shook her head. "Not really. Part of me wants to—it would be great to live near you and the rest of the family again. I spoke to my boss, who said I could easily transfer to the Albany office, but it's such a big decision. I like Denver and have friends there, but . . . oh, hell, I don't know. Mom said she'd move back here if I wanted to—not to live with me, though. She'd find another senior living facility. But if I want to stay in Denver, then she will too. Anyway, I have four weeks before I have to go back to work. Hopefully, I'll know by then what I want to do."

Between her annual vacation allowance and a lot of unused personal time, she'd been able to take a full month off of work to deal with her aunt's estate. That was after the week she'd taken to fly in for the memorial services, which her aunt had pre-arranged at some point with a local funeral home and the church she'd attended most of her life.

Sadie wrapped her arms around Allie in a comforting hug. "You'll make the decision when the time is right. I'll support you either way. I'd love to have you and your mother back here, but you have to do what's best for you." Releasing her, Sadie grabbed her purse and keys from the coffee table. "All right. I have to go pick up Jayne and take her to soccer practice. Call if you need anything else or think of something we forgot."

"I will."

"Are you sure you don't want to come over for dinner tonight?"

She waved her cousin off. "Yeah, but thanks anyway. I'll grab something at the hotel, then stop at the supermarket and pick up some food on my way here tomorrow. At least the refrigerator is clean now." It'd been the first thing they'd worked on when Sadie had arrived earlier. Thank God the electric bills were on auto-pay, so it hadn't been too disgusting to throw out everything in the freezer and fridge that'd been there for at least two months before scrubbing the interior.

After Sadie left, Allie called her mother, who picked up on the second ring. "Hi, sweetheart. I was just thinking about you. How's it going?"

"Okay, I guess. Sadie was here for a few hours, and we've made a battle plan to attack everything that needs to be done."

"I wish I could be there to help." Her mother, Brenda, had tripped and fallen last week, breaking her left wrist. Instead of taking another trip back east with

Allie, she'd stayed home since there would've been little she could do one-handed. Allie's father, Patrick, had died a few years ago. Since then, her mom had sold their house and moved into an apartment in a senior living complex where she had plenty of friends who could assist her.

"We've got it covered. Sadie is bringing Pete, Jayne, and Matt over on Saturday, along with two of Matt's friends. The boys can help Pete sort through the things in the basement and garage while Sadie, Jayne, and I tackle all the closets and stuff."

Matt and his friends were all thirteen years old, while his younger sister was eleven. Allie planned to pay the kids for their time and then get Sadie and Pete a gift certificate to a nice restaurant or something since they would never accept money from her.

"Are you staying there tonight or at the hotel again?"

"Aunt Em bought a new full-size mattress for the spare bedroom at some point—it's still wrapped in the plastic it was delivered in, so she must've recently gotten it. She only had that old blue quilt on it. There are linens in the closet, but I don't know when she washed them last, so I ran them through the laundry earlier. Tomorrow, I'm going shopping for a few things, and pillows and a comforter are on my list. I'll sleep at the hotel again tonight since it's too late to check out, but I'll stay here starting tomorrow."

She'd flown into Albany yesterday, picked up the SUV she'd rented, and driven to Holden, where she'd checked into a hotel not far from her aunt's house. While Emily had kept her home clean, it'd been two months since anyone had been in it. Allie had decided to wait until she and Sadie could take a quick inventory of what they needed and give everything a good scrubbing before she moved in for the next few weeks. In addition to the kitchen, they'd cleaned both bathrooms earlier.

"Okay. Good."

She paced the living room. "How are you feeling? How's the arm?"

"Better. I didn't need the pain pills today. Tylenol was enough. Margie will be here in about ten minutes to take me to lunch, so don't worry about me."

After a little more chitchat, they ended the call. Her mom had such wonderful friends in Denver, which was one of the reasons Allie was waffling on whether to move back to Holden. It wasn't as if Brenda couldn't make new friends—in fact, she still stayed in touch with several from when she'd lived in New York.

"Ugh. You won't figure this out tonight," Allie said aloud.

Making sure she had the list Sadie had given her,

she gathered her purse and the keys to the rented Toyota. Two hours later, the rear of the SUV was stocked with storage totes and bags filled with everything she needed. Arriving at the hotel, she pulled up to the valet parking, thankful she didn't have to empty the vehicle since they had a secure lot for their guests.

When a uniformed young man opened the door, she climbed out. "Is there a quiet place within walking distance where I can get a good burger or something?"

The hotel had an excellent restaurant, but it was pricey. Thirty-five dollars for a cheeseburger and fries was too much.

Holden had grown tremendously since she'd lived there, and most of the town didn't seem familiar to her anymore. Many new malls, shopping centers, office buildings, housing developments, and condo complexes were added. A minor-league ballpark was built on the outskirts of town and was now home to an AA team affiliated with the Yankees. Her old high school was in the same place, but another building had been added, doubling its size. There were still businesses she recognized from long ago, but those were few and far between.

The valet pointed toward the end of the street. "Stay on this side and go past the traffic light. Another half block down, there's a great place called the Cat &

Fiddle. The food is awesome, and it shouldn't be too crowded since it's Tuesday."

"Thank you." She tipped him when he handed her a claim stub.

Glancing down at her T-shirt and jeans, she frowned when she saw how dirty they'd gotten throughout the day. Smudges of dust and grime were too noticeable for her to be out in public, so she headed into the hotel and took the elevator to her room.

Thirty minutes later, she was scrubbed clean after a wonderful spa-style shower and dressed in black capris, a celery-green V-neck top, and black canvas shoes. A light application of blush, eyeliner, and lip gloss enhanced her facial features. Her hair was still damp but clipped into a messy yet stylish knot. It was so thick that she usually let it air dry for a while before blowing it out unless she was in a rush. When that happened, her arms tended to ache from holding the dryer and brush by the time she was done. Putting her hair up was the easiest option tonight since she was hungry and eating alone.

It was a beautiful mid-spring evening, with a temperature of sixty-eight degrees according to a weather app on her phone, so the walk from the hotel was enjoyable, and it didn't take long to arrive at her destination. It sat between a hair salon and a small bookstore. A hunter-green awning complemented the pub's rich dark wood exterior. Above that, an image of a cat playing a fiddle and the establishment's name were carved into a large, decorative wooden sign. The place was inviting, and had she just come across it, she probably would've chosen to eat there even without the valet's recommendation.

Glancing upward at the rest of the building, she noticed what appeared to be four floors of apartments. It was in a nice area and not too far from the train station, and she briefly wondered what the downtown rents were in Holden nowadays. The main streets had been updated over the years, and attractive lampposts, flower beds, and trees now lined the outer edges of the sidewalks. Older buildings had been replaced by newer ones, or their facades had gotten facelifts. It wouldn't be a hardship to live there again if she decided to move back.

Opening the door, she strode in and found the restaurant's interior was just as pleasant—cozy and welcoming. The valet had been right. It was quiet, although a few customers were scattered among several tables while others were sitting at the long, elaborate bar that seemed to be made from the same wood used for the front facade.

Not wanting to sit alone at a table, Allie took a stool at the bar, leaving several empty ones between herself and two older men watching a sports channel on a TV above the shelves filled with liquor bottles. At the far end, a lone bartender had his back to her as he prepared drinks for a waiting server. Beyond that was the entrance to the kitchen and a hallway that probably led to the bathrooms. Opposite the bar were two openings to another room, one at the front of the restaurant and the other at the back. She peeked through the closest one, and the room appeared to be another dining area. It was probably used for parties or overflow on busy nights.

A small bar menu was propped up in a holder in front of the seat next to her, and she snatched it, hoping to find something that sounded good enough to order. However, she was so famished that she would eat practically anything. She'd had breakfast around 8:30 a.m. before heading over to Aunt Emily's and nothing since, except a few bottles of water and a granola bar she'd brought with her.

While she was perusing the menu, a coaster slid across the bar and landed in front of her. A deep, rumbling voice said, "Hi, welcome to the Cat & Fiddle. Can I get you something to drink?"

Her gaze lifted, and her jaw nearly hit the floor as she prayed her mind was playing tricks on her.

Holy shit! No, it can't be. Please, no.

But it was. She'd recognize that handsome yet devilish face anywhere, even after all these years.

Weston Lockhart. Her former crush and the source of a teenage humiliation that still stung almost two decades later. Her heart squeezed painfully at the memory.

As much as she hated to admit it, he'd aged well. He was taller than she recalled—his shoulders were broader, too—but that was to be expected considering they'd both been fifteen the last time she saw him. His jet-black hair now had a touch of gray at the temples, and his eyes were still cobalt blue. They were piercing, and it took a moment for her to realize they were aimed directly at her face, but she saw no sign of recognition. Of course, he wouldn't remember her. She doubted anyone from Holden High would since she'd been far from popular and left after the tenth grade.

When his eyebrows inched upward, she couldn't bring to mind what he'd asked her. "Um, I'm sorry. I zoned out there for a second. It's been a long day."

A smile spread across his face, making him even more attractive. And damn it, he still had those adorable dimples she hadn't forgotten. She would've flirted with him if he was any other man. But her memories of the past squashed that urge in a heartbeat.

"I asked if I could get you something to drink."

Alcohol. Yes, definitely. She needed something to calm the range of unwelcome emotions coursing through her. Glancing at the array of bottles behind the bar, she tried to concentrate on the labels and force herself to relax and act nonchalant. "An old-fashioned with Four Roses, please."

"Coming right up." He pointed to a chalkboard hanging on the wall to her right. "Tonight's specials are listed there. Let me know if you have any questions."

When he turned his back to her, grabbing the bottle of Kentucky bourbon she'd requested, her shoulders sagged, and her stomach roiled. She muttered the famous line from *Casablanca* to herself with a slight twist. "Of all the gin joints, in all the towns, in all the world, I had to walk into his."

It was kind of surprising to find him working as a bartender. Not that there was anything wrong with the profession, but he was on the varsity football team as their second quarterback in only his sophomore year. Even then, people had said he was destined to be drafted into the NFL one day. She didn't follow any sports and wondered if he'd gone pro or not. Either way, how had he ended up working in a bar? As far as she remembered, he'd been a better-than-average student in almost every class except science. He only passed chemistry in her final year at Holden because of her help. And how had he repaid her?

Nope. Don't go there.

Her only salvation right now was that he didn't seem to recognize her. If there'd been any hint he remembered who she was, Allie would've hightailed it out of the pub without a backward glance. But then she would've looked like the fool he thought she was in high school.

Ugh! Stop thinking about that! Have a drink, get something to eat, and enjoy the view. Her gaze dropped to his well-formed ass encased in snug black jeans. *No, don't do that . . . ignore him, drink, eat, and then leave and never come back.*

By the time he brought the old-fashioned over and set it in front of her on the coaster, she'd managed to build up her defenses and resolve. She glanced at the specials board and picked the first thing that caught her eye. "I'll have the sun-dried tomato grilled cheese sandwich, please."

She nearly bit her tongue after that last word. *Why should I be polite to him? Because that's how you were raised! Ugh!*

With a nod, he said, "That's one of my favorites. Homemade potato chips or fries?"

"Um, the chips sound good. Thanks."

"No problem."

As he left to place her order, her gaze slid down his back, past his trim waist, to that fine ass again. Silently cursing, she picked up her drink and took a large gulp.

Chapter 4

As West tried to keep an eye on his other patrons' drinks, his waitstaff, and things being said to him, the pretty auburn-haired woman at the end of the bar kept stealing his attention. The moment she walked in, he'd noticed her. She was about his age, maybe five inches shorter than his own six-foot-one. Her shapely frame was toned but thick enough to garner his interest. Skinny women didn't do it for him. They never had. Even as a teen, he'd lusted after the curvaceous girls in school—and if they were smart, that made them even more attractive to him.

When he studied the woman while she decided what to drink, he had a vague sense of having met her before but couldn't figure out where or when. There was no way she'd ever been to his pub—at least not on a night when he was there—because he definitely would've remembered her. Holden had grown three-fold since he'd been in high school, and while he still knew many people there, plenty of residents were unknown to him now. However, strangers occasionally recognized him from his NFL days.

There was a mid-western lilt to the woman's voice when she spoke, so maybe she was new to the area or visiting someone. But why was she alone? Someone that delectable shouldn't be dining by herself.

After he took her order and walked away, she pulled an iPad out of her purse and started reading. It must not be anything good because she frowned several times. Every once in a while, she glanced in West's direction but then quickly returned her attention to the device. He hoped she wasn't one of those customers who got impatient when their meal wasn't served three minutes after they ordered it.

Out of the corner of his eye, West observed her, trying to figure out where he might know her from and why she wasn't with anyone. There wasn't anything wrong with eating alone—people did it all the time at the Cat & Fiddle—but a woman that beautiful had to be beating guys off with a stick. He hadn't seen a ring on her left hand or the faded skin coloring that said one had been recently removed. It was one of the first things he checked for nowadays when a lady piqued his interest.

Owning a popular pub allowed him to meet many women, but that wasn't always a good thing. Many came there searching for a one-night stand, a quick weekend fling, or a boyfriend they would need to hide from their husbands. He found that out the hard way once when he unknowingly hooked up with a thirty-year-old woman who forgot to mention she was married until after they'd gotten down and dirty. The next day, the cops needed to intervene when her husband showed up at the restaurant, demanding to know which bartender had fucked his wife in the office the night before. The guy started tearing up the bar when he didn't get an answer and was eventually arrested. Yup. Not West's finest hour, but that was more than a few years ago and made him more wary of who he got involved with.

The days of not minding a revolving door full of women were long gone. West wanted what several of his friends had found—someone he could spend the rest of his life with. He'd always wanted to be a father, too, but none of the relationships he'd had over the years had worked out. There was always something missing, but he'd never been able to figure out what.

Wandering down the bar, he checked everyone's drink before stopping in front of her. "Can I get you a refill?"

Her glass was almost empty, and she seemed

surprised when she glanced at it. "Um, no. I'll take a club soda with a twist of lemon, thanks."

He could get that without stepping away from her and quickly filled a Collins glass with ice. "I'm sorry, but have we met someplace before?"

Her green eyes widened a bit. "Uh . . . n-no. I don't think so. I'm from Colorado—Denver. I'm in town settling my aunt's estate."

"Oh, I'm sorry for your loss."

"Thank you." She seemed flustered, as if she hadn't expected his sympathy.

He tossed a new coaster next to the old-fashioned and set the non-alcoholic drink on it. For some reason, he didn't want to walk away yet. He was drawn to her like a moth to a flame. As he dried his hands on a nearby towel, he said, "I'm West Lockhart, by the way. This is my pub."

Her brow furrowed. "Really? I mean . . ."

When she didn't finish the sentence, he did it for her. "Why am I bartending if I own the place?" He smiled and gave her a wink as chagrin filled her pretty face. "I didn't take that as an insult if that's what you're worried about. I like working behind the bar, especially on quieter nights. It gives me a break from all the paperwork that goes into running this place, and I get to meet new and interesting people, such as yourself."

Yup, he was flirting with her—he couldn't help

himself. Something about this woman intrigued him, and he didn't know why since they'd only met less than ten minutes ago. Hell, he hadn't even learned her name —yet.

Pink stole across her cheeks, and his cock twitched at the sight. He wondered if other parts of her body blushed that prettily when she was aroused. More blood rushed to his groin at the thought of her naked in his bed. He shifted his hips, thankful that the bar was high enough to hide his semi-hard-on until he could get it under control.

As he tried to think of something else witty to say, two *dings* resounded from the kitchen, alerting him that her meal was ready. "I'll be right back."

GET IT TOGETHER, ALLIE. REMEMBER WHO THIS MAN *is and how he tried to embarrass you in front of the* entire *school.*

Anger and indignation rose to the forefront of her mind, pushing aside the attraction and desire that had bubbled up inside her when he smiled and winked at her. Without a doubt, he was flirting with her, something he probably did with every adult female who walked into the place. What would he say if he found out who she really was? Would he still smile and talk to her, or would that handsome face fill with disgust at the memory of the plump, nerdy, four-eyed teen she'd been back then?

But he doesn't recognize you, girl. Wouldn't it be fun to flirt, get him all hot and horny, then walk out without a backward glance? Get a little retribution for his attempt to humiliate you?

She'd never been a cocktease before, but suddenly, the idea was tempting. Very tempting.

As West sauntered the length of the bar toward her, carrying what appeared to be her dinner, she couldn't deny that her mouth watered, and it wasn't because of the food. His gaze was focused on her, its intensity making her wet. She forced herself not to squirm to relieve the sudden ache of desire pulsating through her clit. *Holy shit*—the bastard shouldn't have that effect on her, but he did. It was more intense than anything she'd ever experienced.

A pair of one-night stands in her past had both left her somewhat sated yet lonely. The lesson learned was that she would rather get down and dirty with her vibrator than someone she would never see again. She usually waited until after at least three dates before she slept with a guy. There had been several boyfriends during and after college, the longest lasting three years, but they'd all eventually moved on for one reason or another. She'd ended the lengthier relationships after finally admitting that, while she liked and possibly loved those men, she hadn't been *in* love with them. She hadn't been able to see herself spending the rest of her life with any of them.

Maybe she was destined never to marry. The thought saddened her because she'd always dreamed of finding someone to love, have children, and grow old with. However, she refused to spend a lifetime with a man without her whole heart and soul involved. There would be no settling for her. It was all or nothing.

Well, whatever her future held, it certainly didn't include Weston Lockhart, but when he grinned as he set the full plate, a napkin, and utensils in front of her, she almost wished it did. If he were still the boy she'd had a crush on before he tried to embarrass her, then maybe she would've given him a chance, but right now, all she could think of was getting sweet revenge.

The more the notion rattled around her mind, the more she liked it. He might not figure out that she was exacting a little payback, but *she* would know, and that would be satisfying enough.

"Thanks. Mmmm, yummy," she purred before she intentionally licked her lips. She almost smirked when she noticed West's interested gaze follow her tongue.

The sandwich *did* look and smell delicious, and she picked up one half and took a small bite. Her eyes rounded in delight when the first morsel hit her taste buds. The combination of brioche bread, different cheeses, and sun-dried tomatoes perfectly complemented each other. According to the description on the specials board, the cheeses were Gouda, Swiss, and Colby Jack.

"Like it?" West asked as he set a glass with a piece of paper in it on the bar—presumably her tab.

Nodding, she chewed, then swallowed and used her napkin to wipe her mouth. "Like it? I love it! I've never had grilled cheese with anything else on it before, but this is amazing."

"Glad to hear it. It's always popular when we list it. My chef and I have been thinking of updating the menu, and we might put that on it permanently instead of having it as an occasional special."

"You really should. This is the best grilled cheese I've ever had." It was the truth.

His dimples appeared again. "With that endorsement, consider it done." When a server at the other end of the bar called his name, West pointed at Allie's sandwich. "Enjoy. I'll be back in a few to check on you."

Once again, her gaze strayed to his ass as he walked the bar's length. Flirting with him didn't seem like it would be a hardship. He was still easy on the eyes, but retaliation was Allie's main focus.

Chapter 5

After filling a few drink orders for the waitstaff and then tending to a foursome who'd sat at the bar, it took a little longer than he hoped before West could return to the auburn-haired beauty. Thankfully, she was still there when his Tuesday night bartender, Max Abrams, hurried in from the kitchen since most staff members parked in the building's rear lot.

"Thanks for covering for me, boss." Max tossed his car keys into a utility drawer behind the bar under the rows of liquor bottles and set his cell phone next to one of the registers. Usually, West didn't like his employees having their phones out in view of the customers. However, he recently made an exception for Max since the young man's mother was in the hospital recovering from brain surgery to remove a small cancerous tumor.

If there was an emergency, one of the nurses would contact him, and it was easier for them only to have his cell number listed to call.

"No worries. How's your mom doing?"

"Okay, I guess, but tired. The biopsy results came back, and it was as they expected, so for now, she doesn't need the chemo, only radiation. The doctor thinks they removed all of it based on the latest MRI. A physical therapist got her out of bed this afternoon, down the hallway, and back using a walker. She did pretty well, but it took a lot out of her. When I left, she was sound asleep. If all goes well, they might release her to the rehab facility on Friday and start the radiation in a few weeks."

West patted him on the shoulder. "That's great news. I'm sure she'll be glad to get out of the hospital. Let me know if you need any more time off or some swaps with anyone."

"I will, thanks. Oh, and Mom told me to thank you for the soup. She ate it all." After West's suggestion when they spoke last night, Max had stopped by around noon to get a container of the soup of the day to bring to her.

"Probably since it wasn't hospital food. Glad she liked it."

Before letting Max take over the rest of the shift, West gave him a quick rundown on the customers sitting at the bar, whether they'd ordered food or not, and the status of their tabs. Once that was all settled, he grabbed a bottle of his favorite locally brewed ale, circled around to the other side of the bar, and sat next to the attractive woman whose name he still didn't know. When Max removed her now-empty plate and asked if she wanted a fresh drink, she glanced at West before pushing her club soda aside and ordering another old-fashioned. West hoped that meant she was sticking around for a while because he found her fascinating despite not knowing anything about her.

"Are you done for the night?" she asked him as the bartender mixed her drink.

"Yup. Max had some personal stuff to take care of today, and I was covering until he arrived."

"That was nice of you."

He smiled and shrugged. "I'm always nice, um . . ." He paused and eyed her. "You never told me your name."

Her brow furrowed. "I didn't? I'm sorry, I'm Allie— uh, Allie McKenna."

The name didn't sound familiar at all, but the more he studied her, the more he thought they'd met before. However, his mind was blank on where and when it might have been. But that didn't mean he couldn't get to know her now. He held out his hand, and she met him halfway.

"Well, it's nice to meet you, Allie McKenna. Will you be in the area long, or are you heading back to Colorado soon?"

"Um, I'll be here for a few weeks. My aunt was a bit of a hoarder—a neat one, but it's a three-bedroom house, and I have to go through a lot of stuff. You know, figuring out what to keep, donate, or sell."

When Max set her new drink in front of her, West told him to put it on the house before turning back to Allie. "That sounds like a big project. I hope you have someone helping you out." *Just not a husband or boyfriend or anyone who wanted to be one or the other.*

"My cousin doesn't live far—she's coming over this weekend with her husband and kids to help sort through some things."

"Well, that's good. Let me know if you need anything, like a dumpster or a storage unit. Thanks to this place, I've made connections with a lot of people in different businesses over the years."

"So far, we have everything covered, but thank you for the offer." She sipped her drink, then asked, "How long have you owned the bar?"

"A little more than a decade. I was a football player in college but knew if I didn't make it to the pros, or if I did and got injured, I would need something to fall back on, so I got a business degree. And I'm glad I did because, although I played for two years with the

Jacksonville Jaguars as their backup quarterback, I got sacked in a game by two guys twice my size and landed on my arm wrong. Tore my left bicep to shreds," he pointed to the old injury, "and that was the end of football. So, I eventually took the money I'd saved and bought this place when the original owner passed away. His widow didn't want to keep it. I kept most of his staff since he'd already made it a successful business."

He realized that was way more information than she'd asked about—for some reason, she was easy to talk to, even though he barely knew her. "Anyway, that's the long answer to your simple question. What about you? What do you do in Denver?"

She smiled, and his dick stirred at the sight again.

"I'M A CPA," ALLIE TOLD HIM, NOT WANTING TO reveal her true career as a forensic accountant with the Drug Enforcement Agency. While not a gun-carrying agent, she worked in an office, tracking the financial transactions between drug dealers and their suppliers. The cartels often laundered money through legitimate businesses, and it was up to Allie and the rest of her team to figure out which ones.

That wasn't the only half-truth she'd told him

tonight—she'd used Sadie's last name to avoid having West put two and two together and realize Allie was the gawky teen he'd known as Allondra Dawson. She'd learned from DEA agents who'd worked undercover that the more truthful you were with a backstory, the less likely you'd slip up and blow your cover. She never thought that bit of knowledge would be useful, but now she was glad she had it.

She managed to sidestep his earlier question when he asked if they'd met before, so that technically wasn't a lie. She'd be okay as long as no one from her youth or aunt's funeral walked in and recognized her. That would be completely embarrassing.

"Some people think accounting is boring," she said with a shrug, "but I enjoy my job."

"That's all that matters then, right?"

He held out his beer bottle to her, and she picked up her glass and clinked them together in a nonverbal toast. "Right."

They flirted and chatted for a while—the usual getting-to-know-you stuff that wasn't too personal—and Allie had to keep reminding herself that, despite how sweet West was to her now, it hadn't always been the case.

Her gaze flitted from his beautiful blue eyes to his luscious mouth and back again as he spoke. A five o'clock shadow dusted his jaw and upper lip, and her fingers itched to feel the coarse stubble. He really had aged well. What would it be like to kiss him?

Hmm. Maybe she could take her revenge a step further and find out. That would definitely get him all hot and bothered, and then she could leave him flat—or hard as the case might be.

She sipped her drink before noticing it was refilled again. Was that her third or her fourth? She'd lost count while they'd talked and more customers entered while others left. How long had it been since she finished her dinner and he sat beside her? An hour, at the very least. Despite eating earlier, she was glad she only had to walk the short distance back to the hotel because a nice buzz had settled in her brain. Glancing at his beer bottle, she noted it was also fresh.

A few more drinks. Some more flirting. A kiss or two, and then she'd leave, letting him wonder where the night went wrong and how he'd lost his chance with her. Would he lie awake that night, masturbating to dreams of her? Her nipples tightened and her clit throbbed at the thought. She crossed her legs and tried not to moan as the material of her capris rasped against the tiny bud.

"So, tell me," he said, "why is such an incredible woman like you single? You're smart, beautiful, funny —I don't understand why some guy hasn't snatched you up."

Oh, yeah, he was coming on stronger now. Without a doubt, he was thinking about fucking her, and she had to admit to herself the thought had crossed her mind—more than once. Heck, more than a few times.

She smiled coyly and ran the tip of her finger down his arm, starting from the hem of his shirt sleeve, wrapped snugly around his bulging bicep, to the back of his hand. She had a thing for "arm porn," and he had the goods in spades. "Maybe I haven't found the right guy yet?"

"Well, that's an absolute shame, Allie. The men in Denver must be deaf, blind, or gay."

"All three-hundred-fifty-five thousand and five hundred of them?"

His eyebrows shot up. "You know how many men live in Denver?"

She laughed. "It's an estimate. According to the last census, over seven hundred and ten thousand people live in Denver, so I split that in half."

"Off the top of your head? Wow! I may have a business degree, but I'd still have to take some time to figure that out or at least use a calculator. And I sure as hell wouldn't be able to pull a census count out of thin air. I'm impressed."

"What can I say? I'm a numbers person."

He shook his head as a combination of awe and desire crossed his face. "You're an incredible woman."

"You already said that."

"It bears repeating."

His intense gaze was getting her wet, and she almost asked him to turn up the pub's air conditioning because it was getting terribly warm in there.

"Listen," he said. "Are you doing anything tomorrow night? I'm having such a good time talking to you, and I'd like to take you to dinner."

She couldn't agree to that because, after another night in his presence, she might forget why she was coming on to him in the first place. She wanted revenge—nothing more.

Leaning forward, she whispered in his ear. "Is there any reason we can't continue having a good time tonight? Maybe someplace a little more private?"

Pulling back a bit, she knew she had him when he licked his lips before a seductive smile spread across his handsome face and those damn dimples came out in full force. "No reason that I can think of. In fact, we could go upstairs to my apartment for a nightcap if you want."

"You live upstairs?" She didn't know why that surprised her.

"Yup. I actually own this whole building and the one next door. The hair salon and all the apartments are rentals. I kept three of them for myself right above the restaurant and broke down the walls between them, making one big unit."

He was doing better financially than she'd expected when she first saw him behind the bar—not that it meant a difference either way. Money wasn't what she was after. "Wow, I'd love to see it."

"I'd love to show it to you." He nodded at her glass, which was almost empty again. "Want another to take with you? Or I have some wine and beer up there."

She shook her head, knowing if she had any more alcohol, she might throw caution to the wind and sleep with the damn man. "Actually, I think I should switch back to club soda if you don't mind."

"Not at all." He flagged down the bartender. "Max, a club soda with a lemon twist, and I'll take another of these." He gestured to his nearly empty bottle. It was a brand she'd never heard of, which wasn't unusual since she rarely drank any beer other than Coors Light.

Opening her purse, Allie pulled her credit card out of her wallet and set it next to the glass holding her tab. After delivering their drinks, Max processed her bill and gave her the receipt to sign. She left him a nice tip despite only being charged for the sandwich and one old-fashioned—both of which West had served.

Once that was done, West stood and helped her down from the pub-height chair. He threw twenty dollars on the bar, presumably for Max, before picking up the full glass and bottle and jutting his chin toward the back of the restaurant. "If you don't mind taking the stairs, it's only one flight up."

Before she could think twice about doing something so out of character, she smiled and said, "No problem."

"Great. C'mon."

Chapter 6

After West unlocked and opened the door to his apartment, he gestured for Allie to enter first. A large, open living room, dining area, and kitchen combo greeted her as she glanced around. A short hallway to the left had three doorways, and another to the right had two. Everything appeared neat and tidy, and the decor was definitely masculine. Earth tones made it warm and inviting. A huge flat-screen TV, at least sixty-five inches, was flanked by filled bookcases along one wall. An L-shaped couch and two recliners offered plenty of seating. The dining table could fit six people, and the spotless kitchen was a gourmet chef's dream.

Movement out of the corner of her eye caught her attention. A sleek black-and-white cat sashayed into the room and made a beeline for West, circling him and rubbing against his legs. He set his beer bottle and her glass on the countertop between the kitchen and living room and picked up the cat, which nuzzled his chin and neck. "This is Moe. I found him as a stray kitten in the alley behind the restaurant one night and was going to take him to the no-kill shelter. But before the sun came up, he already decided I was his owner."

"How do you know that?"

West set the animal back on the floor. "He managed to get out of the box I put in the bathroom with a towel and clawed his way up and onto my bed. I woke up with him curled in a ball on my chest, sound asleep and purring away. I figured that meant he claimed me as his own." The cat yowled loudly and stared indignantly at West. "That's his 'Why haven't you fed me dinner yet, slave?' meow. Give me a minute to take care of him."

The corners of Allie's mouth lifted as she turned away, not wanting to admit he'd looked adorable, cuddling with the cat.

Ugh. Don't like him. Don't think he's sweet. Don't do anything stupid, like hope you'll see him again after tonight. Stick with the plan and then forget about him for the rest of your life after you walk out the door.

She wandered around the living room, eyeing the many books, photos, and knickknacks filling the shelves on either side of the TV. Collages of more photos hung on the walls. Allie recognized West's parents and younger sisters in several pictures. Although she'd never personally met them, they'd attended all his high school football games, cheering as loudly as everyone else. A few action photos had been taken during games, and she could see the progression from Pop Warner up through high school, then into college, and finally the pros. In other images, he was mugging for the camera with one or more people at various stages of his life. Aside from his sisters and parents, the others in the photos were probably friends, teammates, cousins, etc. None appeared to be a woman who may have been a girlfriend.

As the sound of kibbles being poured into a bowl filtered in from the kitchen, Allie stopped in front of one picture and frowned. It was twenty years old—from their second year of high school—and she recognized it at once. West stood in the middle of a large group of about forty teens, all soaking wet from the car wash that'd been organized to raise money for the Sophomore Social. At one end of the group, she spotted herself, almost unrecognizable due to being partially hidden behind another girl's head—Allie couldn't recall her name.

While glaring at the photo, she ground her teeth together. Ten days after the car wash, West had invited her to go to the dance as his date. What could've been the most thrilling moment of her life up to that point had, instead, been the worst. It was still painful to think about. When her family left Holden behind a few weeks later, Allie was relieved she would never see Weston Lockhart again. Of course, the gods of the universe had warped senses of humor since she was now in the man's apartment.

Spinning around, she found the ghost from her past standing across the room, staring at her with unmistakable desire in his eyes. He was so fucking handsome and sweet now, and it made his high school betrayal hurt even more. Red rage and undeniable lust combined with the alcohol in her system into a furious maelstrom—one she couldn't control if she tried.

No longer giving a damn about whether it was wrong, she stalked toward him and didn't stop until she threw her arms around his neck and slammed her mouth onto his.

Chapter 7

WEST GRABBED ALLIE'S WAIST AND HELD ON AS HE faltered backward, taking her with him and crashing against the wall. It took a few seconds before he regained his balance and realized she was kissing him like no woman ever had. Moments earlier, he could've sworn he glimpsed anger in her expression when she'd turned around to face him. But it disappeared so fast, morphing into desire. Had he been mistaken? She'd been on him before he could say a single word, but there was no way he was objecting.

The kiss was wet, raw, dirty, and delicious. There was no hesitation from either of them when it came to opening their mouths to let their tongues battle for supremacy. She tasted fruity and spicy from the old-fashioned and, combined with her own unique flavor, it was driving him out of his mind. It'd been a long time since West was with a woman who challenged him sexually, and he loved it. Not that he was remotely submissive—he just admired a woman who was confident with her wants and needs.

Allie was all over him, urging him on by rubbing her chest, torso, and pelvis against his as he leaned against the narrow wall between the foyer and kitchen. With one hand in the thick strands of her hair, he ran the other up and down her back, dipping lower with each pass until he cupped her full ass and squeezed. She moaned and lifted her leg until her knee rested against his hip, and he grasped it to keep it there. As she ground against his hard length, the air around them crackled with electricity and intense passion, making him needier than he'd been in a very long time. His body hummed with desire. If they didn't slow down, he would come in his jeans—something that hadn't happened since he was a teenager.

He'd been a bit surprised she'd countered his dinner offer for tomorrow night with one of her own— one that didn't involve eating anything but each other. Never a man to look a gift horse in the mouth, he'd readily agreed since he hadn't wanted to wait any longer to get his hands and mouth on her. There was something about this beautiful woman that drew him in. She sparked something inside him, and not merely in a sexual way. It sucked she was only in New York for a few weeks, but West was determined that this would not be his only night with her until she returned to Denver. Before she left his bed, he'd make sure they had plans for tomorrow night and every night after that. He wanted to imprint her on his memories and vice versa if that were all they would have after she was gone.

Her mouth left his and nuzzled its way to his ear, sending shivers down his spine. "Bedroom?"

West growled, dipped his knees, grabbed the backs of her thighs, and lifted her. As he carried her to his bedroom, she wrapped her legs around his hips and nibbled on his ear. He kicked the door shut as they passed it to keep the cat out.

Moe wasn't invited to this pussy party.

Releasing his grip, he let her legs slide down his until she was standing again. Immediately, she yanked his shirt from his pants. Reaching behind his head, West clutched a handful of the material and pulled the shirt up and off, tossing it aside.

Their mouths met again, but after a few moments, he paused just long enough to remove her shirt. He dragged his hands up her bare arms, over her shoulders, and down her back, leaving goosebumps in their wake. Her skin was so soft against his calloused palms and fingers, and he couldn't stop touching her right then if his life depended on it. He wanted to map out every scrumptious inch of her body.

She grasped his upper arms, turning him a few steps, then pushed him down onto the bed while she remained standing. He leaned against his elbows, taking in her beauty and letting it drown him. Her fingers popped the front clasp of her bra, and her ample breasts bounced when no longer bridled by the garment. He held his breath as she peeled the lacy emerald piece off, revealing two perfectly dark pink nipples begging for his attention. West palmed his throbbing erection, trying to keep it under control—at least until he was inside her. It could be her mouth, pussy, or ass—as long as her heat surrounded his cock, he didn't care what orifice she allowed him to fuck. He wanted to experiment with each one, finding what made her scream his name in ecstasy as she climaxed.

West bit his bottom lip as he waited impatiently for whatever she would do next. Allie clearly wanted to be in control at the moment, and he was willing to let her —for now. He'd take over when the time was right as long as he was one hundred percent sure she wanted everything he was willing to give her. She didn't come across as a cocktease, but if a woman said no at the last second, West respected that. Yeah, it would be exasperating and hurt like hell if she walked out and left him with a case of blue balls, but he would never force himself on anyone.

Allie undid the button on her capris and lowered the zipper before pushing the garment down her legs as she toed off her shoes. Wearing only skimpy panties that matched the discarded bra, she stepped toward the bed. His gaze roamed her body, not lingering too long on one part, wanting to commit as much as possible to his memory.

As she stopped between his spread knees, she tapped one. "Lift."

When he followed her order, she removed his sneaker and dropped it to the floor. Without waiting for further instruction, he lifted the other leg and let her repeat the act. She moved closer, unbuttoning and unzipping his jeans, giving his aching cock some much-needed breathing room. Leaning down, she set her hands on the bed on either side of his hips, then licked and nibbled her way up his happy trail to his chest. Her fingernails scored his flanks, leaving thin red lines on the tanned skin. God, the woman was going to be the death of him tonight, but what a fucking way to go!

The flat of her tongue scraped across his nipple, sending a shiver down his spine. Moaning at the pleasure coursing through him, West thrust his fingers into her thick hair and held her there, encouraging her to tease him some more. He almost shot his load right then when she bit down lightly on the taut peak. His brain was mush—nothing mattered at that moment but how Allie was driving him to the brink of insanity with every hedonistic thing she did to him.

Grabbing her ass, he rolled them over until he was on top before pushing off the bed and shedding the last of his clothes. Free of its restraints, his cock slapped against his lower abdomen, almost painfully. He wrapped his hand around it and squeezed until he was sure he wouldn't come before he was inside her. He eyed her from head to toe, then zeroed in on her panties. That little scrap of material was the only thing standing between them—but not for long.

"Take those off," he demanded, his voice rough with want and need.

Allie rose and slowly stripped before kicking the piece of lace aside. She stared at his cock, making it throb harder in his hand, and then dropped to her knees. *Holy shit!*

Pushing his hand away, she licked his dick from root to tip. West's eyes nearly rolled into the back of his head as he inhaled sharply. She was a beautiful woman to begin with. But seeing her down there, licking her lips as she gawked at his erection like she was starving for it, stunning was the closest word he could use to describe her.

All thoughts fled his mind when she wrapped her

hand and then her lips around him. He was shocked his shaking knees didn't give out as she devoured him. Her tongue tortured him momentarily before she took him to the back of her throat and swallowed around his tip.

"Fuck!" He grasped her hair. "Don't stop. Oh, God, please don't stop. Do that again."

She did it twice more, then bobbed her head up and down as she gave him the best blowjob of his life. With his hand on her head, he urged her to a pace that wasn't too slow or fast. There was no way he would last long in the wet heat of her mouth, but he couldn't resist letting her continue until he absolutely had to stop her.

Allie scratched his bare hip with her manicured nails, leaving more marks he hoped would still be there for days to come.

When he was moments away from orgasm and couldn't take her intense ministrations anymore, he pulled her off him. Her lips were red, wet, and swollen —gorgeous.

"Get on the bed," he growled, releasing her and opening the nightstand's drawer. It'd been a while since he'd had a woman in his apartment, but thank God there was still a box of condoms in there. Pulling one out, he nearly dropped it when Allie got to her feet, turned, and crawled onto the bed like a lioness, showing him her ass and hairless, glistening pussy.

He fucking loved when women were bare down there.

"Stop," he ordered, and she glanced over her shoulder at him. "Spread your knees. Good. Now stay right like that."

After tossing the condom onto the bed, he bent over and clutched her hips. Using his thumbs, he spread her ass checks. "Drop your shoulders and head down."

When she complied, she was in the perfect position for him to feast on her. Her slit was weeping already, and he leaned in for a taste, running his tongue up its length.

"Ah! Oh, shit, WWWWest!"

He chuckled at how his name came out of her mouth like a combination of a whine and a prayer. "Like that, huh?"

Not waiting for a reply, he plunged his tongue inside her, fucking her with it before nibbling on her outer lips. She squirmed closer, encouraging him to eat her, and who was he to deny a woman who expressed what she wanted?

Her moans and pleas mixed with the wet sounds of his licking and sucking. Taking a chance, he moved to the little rosette between her ass cheeks and ran his tongue over it. Her squeal was so loud that he prayed his neighbors hadn't heard her. Her asshole was tight, and he wondered if anyone had ever taken her there. Hopefully, he would be the first if she let him, but for now, he wanted to get into her sweet pussy.

Moving a hand between her legs, he found her clit and rubbed it with two fingers while he retrieved the condom with his other hand. Using his teeth, he ripped open the package and, with a skill he developed over the years, rolled the latex onto his shaft.

"Please, West! Oh, please hurry!"

"On my way, sweetheart. Hang on."

Gripping her hips, he pulled her toward him, bringing her head back up. She braced herself as he aligned the tip of his cock with her entrance and then eased inside. Despite being wet and willing, she was also so damn tight. West clenched his jaw and fixated on where they were joined as he withdrew and thrust in again, gaining ground with each pass.

"Oh, God!" Allie's hands clutched the comforter. "More!"

He gave it to her, pounding into her faster and harder as she rocked against him in time to his pace. Tension and anticipation raced through every cell of his body. This was beyond sex for him—it was more like a sacred experience, unlike anything he'd ever known.

Her cunt squeezed him, and he closed his eyes. Flashes of colored lights appeared behind the lids.

Gasps, moans, groans, muttered curses, and the sounds of flesh slapping against flesh filled the room. Perspiration slicked their heated skin.

Wanting to see her face as she came, West pulled out, grabbed her legs, and flipped her onto her back. He was inside her again within seconds, with his hands on either side of her head, supporting his weight. Her lavish breasts bounced as her hips rose to match every thrust of his cock. Bending down, he kissed her, letting her taste herself on his lips and tongue. Their mouths dueled for dominance, neither one winning.

West couldn't get enough of her. Never before had a woman owned him—mind, body, and soul—as Allie did at that moment.

His orgasm built, but he refused to go over until she went first. Leaning on one hand, he brought the other to her clit and massaged it with short, rapid strokes. "Fucking come for me, Allie. Take me with you."

"Yes! Yes!" She writhed beneath him, her cries of bliss getting louder. To hell with the neighbors. He wanted to hear her scream his name at the top of her lungs.

Her inner muscles quivered around him seconds before the orgasm claimed her. Hot fluid gushed from her core, coating his cock, their legs, and the mattress. "West!"

He drove into her once, twice, and then a third time before he stiffened and followed her into the abyss. Euphoria flushed through him as his cum filled the latex barrier until he was finally spent.

West wasn't aware of how much time had passed before he caught his breath and his brain came back online. It'd short-circuited on him. The woman had undone him in a way no other had, and he prayed it wouldn't be the last time it happened.

Chapter 8

West realized two things before he opened his eyes. One, he was alone in the bed since he was splayed across it, leaving only enough room for Moe if the cat had forgiven him for being locked out last night. And two, it was way past dawn because the glaring sun was hitting his face through his bedroom window because he forgot to shut the blinds last night. Not that anyone could blame him since he'd been so focused on the woman who'd rocked his world.

The woman who was now gone.

Shifting closer to the edge of the bed and rolling onto his side, he stared at the now-vacant spot where Allie had curled up next to him while he succumbed to sleep after a second round of sex in the shower. The silence in the large apartment was deafening, confirming she wasn't in any of the other rooms.

Hoping she'd left a note with at least her phone number, he checked both nightstands and came up empty. After a pit stop to the bathroom, he searched the living room, kitchen, and foyer, the only places that made sense for him to find anything from her, but there was nothing.

Crap.

He got it—really, he did. She was only in Holden for a few weeks and probably had a shit-ton of things to do before returning to Denver. That didn't help him feel any better. For the first time in years, he was crushed over a woman. It had only happened once before, but that had been worse than this—his heart had been heavily invested back then, only to get shot down.

At least, this time, he'd only known Allie for a few hours—but they'd been the best few hours he could ever remember spending with a woman. Sure, over the years, some had slipped out his door after some great sexual gymnastics, while others had lingered far longer than they'd been welcome. However, never once had he been so disappointed the morning after. He hated to admit it, but his heart ached over the fact she was gone without a way to contact her.

Flopping onto the couch, he rested his head on the back cushion and sighed. Allie had it all—beauty, intellect, sensuality, a sense of humor, a great personality, and a good ear. She'd listened as much as she'd talked last night in the bar, and he'd been looking forward to having more discussions with her over the next few weeks before taking her back to his bed.

As Moe hopped on the couch beside him, West leaned forward, opened the laptop that'd been sitting on the coffee table, and spent the next ten or fifteen minutes searching social media and other sites for Allie McKenna with no luck. Well, he did find dozens of women with that name or a similar first name, such as Allison, but none were his Allie. He also searched recent obituaries in the local newspaper for anyone with the last name McKenna, hoping it was also her aunt's surname, but the only person that popped up had been a John McKenna.

When his phone pinged with a message from one of his tenants that she had gotten locked out of her apartment, West finally gave up hope of finding a trace of Allie on the internet. It seemed as if he would only see her again if she decided to return to the Cat & Fiddle. If she did, he'd be waiting for her with bells on. For now, he had work to do.

ALLIE STARED AT THE CEILING IN THE DARK SPARE bedroom for the second morning in a row. It was a little after five a.m., and she'd been awake for about an hour. She couldn't stop thinking about West and how he'd rocked her world the other night. Sex had never been as amazing with anyone as it had been with him, and she hated that it would never happen again. Damn it. Why did it have to be West Lockhart who ruined her for any other man? Of the millions of available men in the world, why him?

After their first round of mind-blowing sex, she cuddled up to him despite knowing she should get dressed and run. But he'd been as sweet and caring as he'd been all those years ago before he tried to play that cruel joke on her. She wished that incident wasn't etched into her memory because she could really fall for the man he was now.

Nope. Not happening. You had your fun, and you'll never see him again. Get over it.

She threw the covers off in disgust and stumbled to the bathroom, knowing she wouldn't get any more sleep no matter how much she tried. A quick shower followed by a stop at a local twenty-four-hour diner for breakfast would kill enough time before the town's Home Depot opened. Over the past two days, she'd distributed the last of the death certificates and run a bunch of other errands on her long list of things to do. After that, she'd tackled the contents of the kitchen pantry and bathroom cabinets, keeping what was needed and discarding the rest.

Once that was all done, she'd sorted through her aunt's walk-in closet full of clothes. Bags and bags of dresses, coats, shirts, pants, shoes, and more were now ready to be donated to a local women's shelter. The total haul would probably take up all the spare room in her SUV, but they didn't open for donations until 11:00 a.m. Until then, she needed to do something to take her mind off West, so she decided to get some paint and supplies to give both bathrooms a new coat. She was still uncertain about moving back to Holden or selling the house, but the interior and exterior needed sprucing up either way. She would probably hire a professional for some of the larger rooms, but she had no problem tackling the smaller ones herself. She'd be there for three and a half more weeks, and sitting around, contemplating the one man she didn't want to think about, would drive her crazy.

During breakfast, Allie perused the local newspaper and did the daily crossword puzzle while drinking a third cup of coffee. The extra caffeine would give her sleep-deprived mind and body the energy needed to get through the day. Hopefully, she'd be so exhausted that night she could stay asleep until at least dawn. She would need plenty of rest for when the troops arrived in the morning to help with everything that still needed to be done.

A little while later, she stood in the paint department at Home Depot, staring at dozens of squares in various colors, trying to narrow down her choices. After walking around her aunt's home for the past several days, Allie was sick of all the white walls and wanted to bring some subtle color into the rooms. In her own condo, she'd painted several whole rooms or accent walls with muted or vibrant colors to brighten things up. To her, plain white was just so *blah*.

It took some time, but she was down to three versions of pale green for the hall bathroom after about fifteen minutes or so. The samples were similar, yet several shades off from each other. A nearby display let her see how each color would manifest in the sunlight and under different variations of light bulbs, but she still couldn't make up her mind.

"Need a second opinion?"

She startled at the voice coming from over her right shoulder, and a shiver went down her spine as she recognized the deep timbre. Spinning around, she came face to chest with West Lockhart. He stood only a few inches from her, and she had to step back to see his face without tilting her chin too far up.

Damn, he was more handsome today than he'd been the other night. Clean-shaven and dressed in well-worn jeans, construction boots, and a snug red T-shirt that hugged every chiseled section of his torso, he made her mouth water. He epitomized the perfect male form, and she wished she was an artist who could sketch or sculpt his body.

"Uh, h-hi. Um, what are you doing here?"

With a twinkle in his eyes, he shrugged nonchalantly and then pointed at three large tin cans on the floor by his feet. "Apparently, the same thing you're doing—picking up some paint. Although, I'm going with an off-white color. One of my tenants moved out, and I have to do a little updating before listing the apartment again." He gestured to the samples she was still holding. "What about you? Painting your aunt's house?"

She licked her lips, and his eyes flared as his gaze followed the motion. "Um, yeah. It hasn't been done in years, so I thought I'd brighten it up before bringing in a realtor." Not that she'd decided to sell the place yet, but he didn't have to know that.

What are the freaking odds of running into him like this? The goddesses of Fate must have it in for her. Do something for the wrong reasons, no matter how much fun it'd been, and they shoved it in your face as a ghastly reminder instead of letting it fade into the past.

"Good idea." He paused for a moment while

scratching his temple. "Um, I had a great time the other night and was disappointed to wake up alone."

Regret filled her as she remembered how much she'd wanted to stay and wake up beside him for morning sex. The most idiotic thing she'd done was not tell him who she really was when she introduced herself to him. If he'd recognized her and not been interested in her, then she wouldn't have experienced the most incredible night of her life. She also wouldn't have known what she missed out on. Now that she did, her penance was that she could never tell him the truth. "Uh, yeah. Sorry—"

He held up a hand, cutting off her automatic apology. "I understand. You're only here for a few weeks before heading back to your life in Denver. Why start something you can't finish, right?"

She nodded, taking the easy out he was giving her. "Exactly. I'm not into one-night stands, just so you know, but I . . . felt a connection with you." That was true, but explaining further was out of the question.

"I sensed it too. In fact, I was kicking myself for not getting your number. Running into you here is like fate, though." He ran a hand through his thick, dark hair. "Listen, I understand your time in Holden has an end date, but I'd really like to get to know you better while you're here. Can I take you out to dinner tonight?"

Her eyes widened. That was the last thing she'd expected him to ask.

"You don't have to say yes," he quickly added. "But it's been a while since I've been with a woman who is as fascinating, funny, and entertaining as you are, and I'd like to enjoy some time with you while I can. We don't have to sleep together again if you don't want to, but I'd be interested in that, too, if you are. I . . . I really liked being with you the other night, and not only in bed."

Placing a splayed hand on his chest, he raised his brows and appeared to be holding his breath as he awaited her response. The wistfulness she saw in his eyes shattered her resolve to avoid him. She couldn't turn him down, no matter how much she should. "I-I'd like to see you again too. Dinner would be nice."

He exhaled in obvious relief. "Great! Um . . . I have to cover for one of my bartenders until five-thirty at the latest. Why don't you come to the bar around five fifteen? As soon as I can get out of there, we'll walk up the street to Blue Danube. It's a steakhouse owned by an older couple who moved to Holden a few years ago. I became friends with them, and we eat at each other's place every now and then."

At least she didn't have to worry about the owners recognizing her. Hopefully, she and West wouldn't encounter anyone they knew from school. Although, if

West still didn't recognize her, it was doubtful anyone else would after all that time.

"That sounds great. I'll see you around five-fifteen."

A grin spread across his handsome face before he pointed at one of the three samples Allie was still holding. "Throwing my two cents in—that's my choice." He picked up his paint cans and stepped backward, still smiling broadly. "I'll see you later, Allie."

"Bye, West."

She stood there, staring at his retreating back until he disappeared around the end of the aisle. Although shaking her head at the stupidity of agreeing to go on a date with him, she couldn't deny that she was excited about it.

Glancing down at the paint samples, she decided his choice was the right one. *Damn it.*

Chapter 9

Sitting at the bar the next night, Allie took a sip of the soda West had given her. He wasn't the only bartender on duty—Max, the young man from the other night, was also there—and she could see why. She'd arrived at 5:15 on the nose to find West had saved her a seat—the same one she'd occupied the other night. There'd been a little sign in front of it that said, "Reserved," and as soon as she'd walked in the door, he caught her eye and gestured toward the stool. The place was already three-quarters full, with more people coming in every few minutes. The staff was bustling. According to West, since it was a Friday evening, every seat at the bar would be taken by six o'clock, with people stacked behind them, and there'd be at least a twenty-minute wait for tables.

Since she hadn't packed any clothes suitable for a

date at a nice restaurant, Allie had gone shopping at the mall after she'd left Home Depot. It took an hour and several stores to find a little black dress that fit her perfectly. It wasn't too formal or casual and could be dressed up or down with the right shoes and accessories. She'd also picked up a pair of black-and-silver heels for tonight.

Over her left shoulder, the pub's front door swung open again, and a tall, pretty, dark-haired woman in her mid-twenties rushed in. She was wearing black pants and a royal blue Cat & Fiddle T-shirt. Her hair was damp and pulled up into a ponytail. West's attention immediately diverted from his customers to the younger woman, and Allie didn't like the unwanted flash of jealousy that shot through her gut.

"Well?" he asked the brunette, who stopped abruptly between two men sitting on the long side of the bar. She bit her lip and hung her head, causing West to frown and put his hands on his hips while gaping at her. "Oh, crap, Kate, don't tell me you failed." His tone wasn't one of disappointment—it was more like despair.

Allie saw the woman's smile before she lifted her head. It was obvious she'd been messing with him. "I passed!

West punched a fist into the air. "Yes! I said you could do it!" Reaching back, he grabbed and yanked on the rope hanging from a brass bell attached to the bar's frame. The loud *ding-ding-ding* had everyone in the pub eyeing him. "Ladies and gents, let's hear it for one of Holden's future police officers, Kate Moynahan! She passed her fitness test!"

Shouts of "congratulations" and applause came from the patrons and staff as Kate ran behind the bar to where West stood near Allie and hugged him. "I can't thank you enough for introducing me to Matt and Valerie. If it wasn't for them training me, I don't think I would've passed the push-ups and the run. In fact, I ran my best time ever for the test!"

He squeezed her, then let go and stepped back. "All I did was hook you up with two friends on the force—you did all the work. I'm proud of you. Although, we'll miss you here. What comes next?"

Kate grinned from ear to ear. "Well, it's not official yet, but from what I was told, they're hiring four recruits to send to the academy to replace officers who are retiring this year. Valerie said my name was on the list as long as I passed the fitness test and my physical and psychological exams, which I did. I think the academy starts the third week in June, so I'll graduate right before Thanksgiving."

"So that gives me about six or seven weeks to find a replacement and have you train them."

"Yup. But don't jinx me. Like I said, nothing's official yet." She held up her purse and a small duffel bag. "Let me put my stuff in the office, and then I'll take over for you. Thanks again for filling in for me, West—I wasn't sure how long it would take, and then I had to run home to shower."

"No worries. Take your time. Everything's good."

As Kate hurried to the back of the pub, Allie couldn't help the smile that appeared on her face as West eyed the drink status of everyone at his end of the bar before his gaze stopped on her face. He raised an eyebrow. "What?"

She shrugged and tried to remind herself she was not supposed to fall for the man's charms. He might be nice now, but he'd also been nice in school before he suddenly wasn't. She was just going to enjoy herself and have some great conversation and sex before she moved on.

Yeah, keep telling yourself that.

"You seem very invested in your employees' lives."

"I am." He leaned against the bar. "I'm proud to admit we have a low employee turnover rate here. Most of the staff have been with the Cat & Fiddle for a long time. Heck, when I bought the place, my assistant manager, chef, sous chef, and two daytime servers had been working here for a few years already and stayed on. It's like an extended family—and not just with the employees. I bet I know more about some of my regulars than their own friends and family do. It's like being a priest or therapist, without the celibacy or insurance paperwork."

"It's your outgoing personality," she said, which was true. The man had been friendly and popular in high school, but now, the words she would use to describe him were gregarious and boisterous. He reminded her of Sam Malone, the bar owner in *Cheers*. She loved watching reruns of the sitcom from the 80s and early 90s. It was where everyone knew your name, and the type of place the Cat & Fiddle appeared to be.

Great. Now she would have that theme song stuck in her head all night.

Before he could respond, Kate returned from the office, tugging her ponytail to ensure it was tight. Smiling, she greeted several customers before turning to West. "Okay, boss, give me the lowdown and then get lost."

He grinned and shook his head. "I gotta stop hiring brats."

WEST TOOK A CHANCE AS THEY STRODE DOWN THE street toward Blue Danube and gently grasped Allie's hand. She seemed surprised but didn't pull away.

She was gorgeous in a simple black dress that

stopped just above her knees and heels that added about two inches to her height. The scoop-neck top showed a tempting bit of cleavage. Gold stud earrings and a necklace with an oval locket completed her outfit, and understated makeup enhanced her facial features. Her hair was pulled off her neck and into a bun—one he wanted to mess up by holding her by it while she gave him another blowjob. Thank fuck he'd taken the edge off of his desire for her earlier in the shower. Otherwise, he would've said to hell with dinner and convinced her to go to his apartment for lots of dirty sex. They would need some decent sustenance, though, if it were anything like the other night.

Her gaze took in their surroundings. "It's been a long time since I walked through downtown Holden. Some businesses have changed, but that pizza place has been there for a long time."

"Yeah, I remember going there after Little League practice when I was a kid—so it's definitely been there for at least twenty-five years. The original owner's son took over when the guy retired." He could get so used to this, wandering around Holden with Allie by his side, just talking and enjoying each other's company. "How often do you get a chance to visit?"

She hesitated a moment before responding. "Not as often as I would like. My parents and I occasionally came here for weddings, funerals, and family reunions.

My aunt, who just passed away, visited us in Colorado a lot, and I stay in touch with the rest of my extended family through social media. But I wish I could see them more often—especially my cousin, Sadie. She's like the sister I never had."

"I get it. Being that far away from those you're close to must be hard. Most of my family still lives in the area. My youngest sister—there are three of them—lives about an hour away. It's still close enough for her to come here or for us to go there with little notice. You said your mom's out in Denver with you, right?"

"Yeah. She moved into a sixty-five-plus community after my dad died, and it's only about fifteen minutes from my condo, so we see each other all the time."

"That's great." He brought them to a stop. "Here we are."

Besides his own place, this was his favorite restaurant in the area. Both in their late fifties, Harry and Leslie Finch were the owners. Harry graduated from the Culinary Institute of America in Hyde Park, New York, and his wife held degrees in both business and marketing. Between them, they'd made Blue Danube a huge success. Thursdays through Sundays, it was almost impossible to get a table. Thankfully, he'd texted Leslie yesterday after he left Home Depot, and she'd penciled him in for one of the few tables they reserved for good friends, family members, and the occasional celebrity. People came from all over for Chef Harry's delicacies after he'd made a name for himself at another restaurant, Sweet Basil, they owned in New York City. A few years ago, the couple decided to semi-retire to Holden to be closer to their daughter and her family. While they made biweekly trips to the city to check on Sweet Basil, the staff and executive chef did a great job of running the place for them.

Holding the door open, West let Allie enter before him. Although it wasn't yet six o'clock at the start of the weekend, almost every table was occupied. As always, the atmosphere was serene and appealing. The blue decor complemented the establishment's name. Navy tablecloths covered each table and were topped with shimmering candles, vases with forget-me-nots and baby's breath, elegant glasses, shiny silverware, and bone-colored plates.

The hostess recognized him at once, smiled, and picked up two menus. "Good evening, Mr. Lockhart. Your table is all set. Follow me, please."

She led them to one of the tables by the back windows, where they could enjoy a large landscaped yard with a gazebo and a pond with a fountain in the middle. It all belonged to the Finches, and they often hosted small weddings and other events there.

"Wow, this is beautiful," Allie said as he pulled out a chair for her.

"Isn't it? Wait until it gets darker—the lights will come on outside, and it looks like something out of a fairy tale."

He sat across from her as their waiter approached, wearing black dress pants, a crisp, white button-down shirt, and a sapphire tie. "Good evening, Mr. Lockhart, ma'am. Can I get you something from the bar?"

"Hi, Chris. I'll have a Glenfiddich on the rocks. Allie, would you like an old-fashioned or something else?"

Facing the waiter, she asked, "Do you have a pinot gris?"

"Yes, we have two. King Estate from Oregon, and Franz Keller from Germany."

"I'll have a glass of the King Estate, please."

When Chris left to get their order, West smiled at Allie. "It seems we have a similar taste for wine. That's one of my favorites."

Her face lit up. "I came across it about ten years ago and haven't been disappointed with a single year since."

"Same here."

Throughout their meal, they chatted like old friends, and once more, West got the impression that he knew her from another time and place, but he still couldn't recall when or where. It wasn't as if he would've had many opportunities to meet her since she lived in Denver and only came to New York on rare visits. It didn't matter, though—he would enjoy her company while he could. In a few weeks, she'd be gone again, and all he would have left were the memories of their time together, as disappointing as it was.

He would miss her something awful. Never had he connected with a woman so quickly before. Yeah, some women in the past had held his interest for a while, and a few he'd dated for extended periods. But he'd always known he was only passing his time with them until the relationships fizzled out. With Allie, he didn't want whatever it was between them to go that route. For once in his life, he wanted something more, and it was with a woman he'd barely known for a few days.

Leslie and then Harry stopped by the table to say hello after he and Allie had finished dinner. Both beamed as Allie gushed over what a wonderful meal it had been. And if West wasn't mistaken, Harry blushed under the pretty woman's praise. Before returning to the kitchen, the older man caught West's eye, winked at him, and subtly mouthed the word "keeper." West grinned and nodded because he agreed with him.

"Can I interest you in a nightcap?" he asked Allie after signing for the check and leaving Chris a generous tip for his excellent service, as usual.

"I think you could." Her seductive smile went straight to his groin, causing his cock to twitch. West quickly recited the dishes he and his chef were considering for the new menu in his head to keep his pants from tenting. Something that was difficult to do whenever he was with Allie. He just had to be in the same room as the woman, and desire would hum through him.

Standing, he took her hand and helped her to her feet. Once they were outside, he said, "I have to stop into the pub for a few minutes and make sure everything is running smoothly. I'm pretty sure it is because I didn't get any text messages saying otherwise, but I'd still like to stop in if that's okay."

"That's fine. I don't mind."

Twenty minutes later, West was reassured all was well at the Cat & Fiddle and watched Allie's heart-shaped ass sway as she preceded him up the stairs to his apartment. His hands itched to smack one of the cheeks to see if it bounced like he thought it would. It was too soon into the relationship to try that without discussing her kinks and pet peeves, but that didn't stop him from thinking about it.

Relationship. Sigh. If only he could use that label to describe what was going on between them. But with an end date getting closer by the minute, he would have to settle for words like affair or fling.

Putting those thoughts out of his mind, he unlocked the door and followed Allie inside. Before she could get more than a few steps away, he gently grabbed her elbow, kicked the door shut, then pushed her against the wall. Bending, he brushed his lips over hers, waiting for a response before taking things further. When she wrapped her arms around his neck and opened her mouth, that was all the invitation he needed.

West ravaged her mouth as he cupped one breast before teasing the hard, little bud hiding behind too many layers of clothes. The caveman in him almost ripped the dress from her body in desperation.

"*Meow!*"

The loud, indignant, startling cry had them parting, and they laughed as Moe did figure eights in and around his owner's spread legs. West touched his forehead to Allie's, his lungs heaving for oxygen. "Sorry about that—he gets jealous sometimes."

He glared down at the cat. "Dude, I really have to get you a girlfriend, but for now, you're cock-blocking me. Shoo." Using his foot, he humanely pushed the animal to the side. Moe flipped his tail at them before regally sauntering away from the peasants he thought them to be.

"Bedroom?" West's voice was strangled by lust.

When she nodded, he leaned down, put his arm behind her knees, picked her up, and then cradled her against his broad chest. Allie giggled as he carried her to the bedroom and closed the door behind them. Along the way, the assertive woman took advantage of her current position, nuzzling and nibbling his neck and ears, sending delicious goosebumps skittering across his skin. Already begging for relief, his cock thickened in his pants.

Setting Allie on her feet, West retook possession of her mouth. He sucked her plump bottom lip between his, then licked it, drawing an erotic moan of hunger from her. Their tongues glided against each other, moving from his mouth to hers and back again. He'd only had two drinks during dinner, but now he was getting drunk on Allie.

While he moved them toward the bed, she unbuttoned his shirt before shoving it off his shoulders and down his arms. Grasping the material of her dress, West dragged it up her body and stopped kissing her only long enough so he could completely remove it. His big hands cupped her restrained breasts, running his thumbs over the pebbled nipples with only the thin material of a black lacy bra between them. His gaze roamed over her barely-clad torso before returning to her face. "God, you're beautiful."

Without giving her an opportunity to respond past a blush, his lips met hers again in a punishing kiss. She opened for him without hesitation, and his tongue plundered inside. He pulled her body flush against his and delighted in the fact that they fit together like two pieces of a puzzle. His erection strained against the fly of his pants, twitching against her abdomen and demanding attention.

Her skin was hot and smooth against his, and her palms wandered over his arms, shoulders, chest, and back. West nipped along her jawline to the sensitive spot under her ear. "I want to spend hours worshiping your body."

She rubbed against him like a cat. "Well, what's stopping you?"

His chortle was cut off when her hands slid down to the clasp and zipper of his pants and made quick work of them. As she tucked her fingers under the waistband of his boxer briefs and teased the tip of his cock, West moaned into her neck. Impatient to see her completely naked again, he stepped back and quickly rid them both of their underwear.

Supporting her head and back, West lowered her to the bed and kissed and licked his way down to her breasts, where he laved and sucked her nipples. She shivered and cried out with want and need. Her nails dug into his shoulders, ramping up his own desire. He relished that the wildcat inside her had emerged.

Grinning against her skin, he moved lower. The closer he got to the apex of her thighs, the more she squirmed and moaned. Her legs spread wider as he sank to his knees beside the bed. "Please, West!"

"Mmm. I love it when you beg." He ran his tongue along the crease of her right hip and then the left before he closed his mouth over her clit and sucked hard. Allie's pelvis lurched upward, and she pleaded for more. Using his fingers to part her folds, West feasted on her, savoring her taste and alternating between her slit and the little bundle of nerves above it. The whiskers on his jaw abraded her sensitive skin, but it only seemed to give her more pleasure as she rubbed her thighs against him. Every so often, he lifted his heavy eyelids, his gaze meeting hers. The raging maelstrom of passion he saw in her eyes was mesmerizing, calling to him like a sea siren.

He plunged his tongue into her, then lashed at her clit again as he eased one and then two fingers inside her. Allie fidgeted under him, pushing against his mouth and hand. She grabbed a handful of his hair, pulling it to the point that his scalp burned. West growled but didn't let up his assault. The pain only fueled his raging libido. He found the spot inside her that made her squeal, and her entire body quivered. "Yes! Oh, God, yes! Please! More!"

He stroked her G-spot repeatedly as her words became incoherent, and she thrashed about on the bed. When he bit down gently on her clit, that was all her body could handle as she screamed her release. Her vaginal walls clenched his fingers while cream gushed from her core. Her back bowed as her hands twisted, one still in his hair, the other clutching the comforter. He continued to lick her clit and finger fuck her, letting her ride out the orgasm until it finally ebbed.

West pushed onto his knees, wiped his sopping-wet chin, and sucked his fingers clean. "Best dessert I've ever had."

He crawled onto the bed and claimed her lips again, letting his tongue sweep inside her mouth so she could taste herself on him. Allie wrapped her hand around his aching cock, and he pumped into her fist several times before it became too much for him to handle. Pushing up onto one hand, West reached over and opened the drawer to his nightstand, grabbing one of the condoms.

Within seconds, he was sheathed and back on top of her. "Put your legs around me."

She did as she was told, digging her heels into his ass, urging him to enter her. The tip of his cock eased inside. She was still slick from her orgasm, and it only took him a few short thrusts to bottom out.

Holding himself there for a moment, he asked, "Okay, baby?"

"Yes!" Allie lifted her pelvis, causing him to slip in further, which he hadn't thought possible. His mouth settled on hers again as his hips set a slow but steady pace. Allie moaned and ran her hands over every inch of his skin she could reach. When West changed the angle of his thrusts, she cried out, and he guessed he'd found that sweet spot inside her again. Liquid heat rushed through his veins as West increased the pace. He was moments away from detonating but tried his hardest to hold on a little longer.

A few strokes later, Allie's squeals increased an octave before she yelled out his name. When she went over the edge this time, she took him with her. His bellow of ecstasy reverberated throughout the bedroom —yeah, the neighbors probably got an earful that time. The people in the bar below them might've heard it too. Hell, West didn't care if the entire town knew he'd just had the most explosive sex of his life.

As they floated back down, still joined as close as two humans could be, an unwelcome thought popped into his head. *How are you going to be able to let her go?*

Chapter 10

"ALL RIGHT, WHAT IS UP YOUR ASS TODAY?" SADIE asked Allie after her daughter, Jayne, left the kitchen to use the bathroom.

She tried acting like she didn't know what the other woman was asking. "What do you mean?"

"Don't give me that shit, Allie. You're distracted by something, and it's not Aunt Emily's tea cup collection. You hate tea as much as I do. Now, what gives?"

After a moment's hesitation, Allie checked the dining room and living room to ensure no other ears could hear her. Pete and the boys were in the garage, sorting through the massive amount of stuff there. Biting her lip, she turned back to her cousin. "I screwed up."

Sadie's brow furrowed. "What? How?"

A resigned sigh slipped past her lips. "Do you remember West Lockhart?'

"West Lockhart? Hmm. Why does that name sound famil—oooohhhh." Wide-eyed, she pointed at Allie. "Wait a minute. *West Lockhart!* Wasn't he the guy in your high school you had a huge crush on, who asked you to the dance and—"

"Yup," she interrupted. "And it's humiliating enough without you saying it out loud, thank you very much. Anyway, I ran into him the other night—he owns an Irish pub near the hotel."

"Tell me he's not as hot as you thought back then."

"Ugh, I wish. He's freaking gorgeous, the jerk."

"Okaaaay. Did he recognize you?"

"Nope."

With a furrowed brow, Sadie sat at the kitchen table. "All right, I'm confused. How did you screw up?" Her gaze shifted to something by the doorway to the hall. "Oh, Jayne, go help Daddy for a few minutes —Allie and I need to talk about something."

"Okay, Mom."

Her cousin was right—Allie was so distracted she hadn't even heard Sadie's daughter return. They waited until the door to the garage opened and closed again, and then Sadie leaned forward. "Tell me what happened."

Allie's gaze darted everywhere but toward her

cousin. She should've kept her mouth shut, to begin with, but the other woman had always been her confidante. In fact, she was the only one aware of Allie's crush on West back then. And his betrayal. "I . . . um . . . I kind of slept with him."

"What!" After the initial yell, her cousin quickly lowered her voice. "Are you crazy? You had *sex* with the guy who treated you like shit your sophomore year of high school?"

"It wasn't the whole year," she retorted, trying to salvage some of her dignity. "Just near the end of it."

"Oh, like that makes a big difference after what he did." Sadie paused, frowning and shaking her head. "Okay, let me get this straight. You said he didn't recognize you, so does that mean he doesn't remember you, or at least your name? Did you tell him your name?"

"Um . . . I sort of introduced myself as Allie McKenna." When Sadie opened her mouth to ask another question, Allie held up a hand to stop her. Instead of playing a game of twenty questions, she spent the next few minutes explaining what happened the other night. "I was only going to tease him and then walk away—get my own bit of revenge, even if he didn't know about it. But after a few drinks, things got a little out of hand, and we . . . well, I already said that part." She bit her lip briefly. "But that's not all."

"There's more?" Sadie rolled her eyes. "Of course, there's more. What else?"

"I had dinner with him last night and kind of slept with him again."

Her cousin's mouth opened and closed a few times before she stood and stalked over to the pantry. Despite it only being a little before noon, she grabbed a bottle of vodka that'd been left over from one of Aunt Emily's parties. Finding two shot glasses at the top of one of the donation boxes on the counter, she didn't bother to rinse them out before setting them on the table and filling them. "I knew I should've picked up some Bloody Mary mix on the way over."

Lifting up one of the glasses, Sadie gestured for Allie to do the same.

Oh, what the hell . . .

After clinking them together, both women quickly downed the shots and gasped as the strong alcohol hit their throats.

Sadie sounded like a frog when she spoke again. "Okay, tell me what this is all about." She cleared her throat before continuing. "You've never really been into one- or two-night stands or a cocktease or a revenge fuck kinda girl, so what gives? And why do you sound like you're regretting it all?"

Allie sighed. "Because I am?"

"You're asking me? How the hell should I know?"

"All right, all right. I *do* regret it. But he's different now. I mean, he's like he was before he tried to humiliate me—nice, sweet, and funny—but he's so much more than that now." She flailed her hands as she spoke, as if that would help explain why she'd done something so dumb. "You should see how he treats his staff and customers—like they're all a part of one big family. A close family—like ours. If he were anyone but West Lockhart, I'd be interested in seeing where this goes between us. He's exactly the type of guy I've always wanted to date, but whatever chance I might have had with him is all based on a lie—*several* lies. How can I think of moving back here when there will always be a chance of running into him again and him finding out who I really am?"

Sadie poured them each another shot of vodka, and those went down a lot smoother than the first. "Okay, first of all, do *not* let whatever this is influence whether you move back here or not. I would love to have you living near me again, so take that out of the decision equation. If you do come back, then you'll have to tell him the truth before he finds out because, Allie, he will eventually find out. Yeah, Holden's gotten bigger since you left, but it's still a small town. You'll run into him again sooner or later."

"You're not helping." Allie glared at her. "And it won't matter *when* he finds out, he'll still hate me."

There was a long pause, with only the ticking of Aunt Emily's Betty Boop clock on the wall filling the silence. Finally, her cousin said, "You're falling for him, aren't you?"

Stretching her arms across the table, she gently banged her head against them in frustration. "Yeah, I think I am."

"Then you've got to find a way to tell him the truth and soon. Otherwise, you'll both end up getting hurt."

Unfortunately, it was probably too late for that.

Chapter 11

A LITTLE OVER TWO WEEKS LATER, ALLIE STILL hadn't found the courage to tell West who she really was. With every day that passed, it would only hurt him that much more.

You're a coward—admit it.

They'd gone out on several dates and spent a few other evenings at his place, eating in, watching movies, talking, and, of course, having sex. She and Moe had taken a liking to each other, and the cat greeted her every time with meows and figure eights around her legs. He often sat in her lap, too, which surprised his owner.

West had never questioned why Allie didn't invite him to her aunt's house, but that was probably due to how much she talked about all the filled boxes and loose items scattered about the house and garage. Over the past few weeks, she sorted everything for donations, today's yard sale, and what she wanted to keep.

Allie never thought she could be described as insatiable regarding sex until West came back into her life. But she couldn't get enough of him and hated that they only had one more week together before she returned to Denver. After that, she'd probably never see him again, but he would remain in her mind and heart forever.

The more time she spent with him, the less she remembered the end of their sophomore year at school. Although she would never forget his attempt to degrade her, she no longer hated him. Instead, she'd fallen in love with him. Karma was a cruel bitch.

"Excuse me, how much is this?"

The question dragged her back to reality and the yard sale. Allie stared at the 16" x 20" framed ocean painting that a woman was holding up and rattled off the first number that came to mind. "Two dollars."

The woman's eyes widened at the lowball price, and she immediately said, "I'll take it."

When she handed over the money, Allie stuck it in the back pocket of her jeans.

Sadie had offered to help her today, but Allie had told her not to bother coming over. Two of Aunt

Emily's neighbors had decided to combine forces with her, bringing their own things to sell. All the heavy furniture from her aunt's house had either been donated or sold on eBay and Facebook Marketplace, except for the spare bedroom set, the kitchen table, and a few pieces in the living room so Allie could sit and watch TV. Boxes were being used as end tables for lamps, and an old Army trunk that'd belonged to the uncle she'd never known served as a coffee table. Sadie and Pete would sell the remaining furniture and anything else Allie left behind if she decided to stay in Denver, which was a given now. There was no way West would forgive her when he found out she was lying to him, and the only way to avoid that was to remain in Colorado.

That morning, it'd been easy to set up everything because what she wanted to sell had been stored in boxes and piled in the garage where she could easily drag it out. She'd displayed smaller items atop several folding tables on the driveway and a few old clean sheets laid out on the lawn. Mrs. Marcus and Mrs. Kim had brought over more tables and sheets for their own things, along with folding chairs they'd placed in the shade of a big tree where they could keep an eye on everything. Allie was thankful they decided to join her because she hadn't thought of needing some time for bathroom breaks. A few dishonest people would probably have taken advantage of that and stolen some things.

It was a little before noon, and she'd already sold about three hundred dollars worth of stuff, and there was still plenty more to get rid of. People came and went, some making quick passes to see what she had, while others lingered, inspecting each item before selecting the ones they wanted to haggle over.

Sitting on a lawn chair inside the open overhead garage door, Allie was surprised when she recognized West's dark gray pickup truck parking next to the curb. She had a moment of panic. It was highly unlikely for anyone, including the neighbors, to use her real surname in front of him, so she should be safe about that. But her mind raced through each room of the house, trying to recall if any family photos with her in them had been left out, especially those from her youth. She couldn't risk West seeing them and recognizing her. Relief ran through her when she remembered they were all packed up in the boxes she needed to ship to Denver, along with other mementos and heirlooms she wanted to keep.

Tall and handsome, wearing worn jeans, sneakers, a snug gray T-shirt, and a New York Yankees cap, West garnered appreciative stares from several women and at least two men as he strode up the driveway, heading straight for her. He was carrying a brown paper bag in the crook of his arm. Although the sun was shining, he brightened her day even more.

A thought hit her. While she'd told him she was having the yard sale today, she'd never mentioned her aunt's last name or where the house was, so how had he known how to find her? When they'd exchanged phone numbers a few weeks ago, she'd given him the one from her Google Voice account, which forwarded calls and texts to her cell phone. It was another precaution she'd learned about while working for the DEA, and it often came in handy when she didn't want to give someone her real number.

West stopped in front of her, leaned down, and gave her a chaste kiss on the lips that promised something steamier when they were alone. "Did you know there are at least fifteen yard sales in Holden today? I found that out because yours is the fifteenth one I've stopped at. I tried calling you earlier to see if you needed help, but it went to voicemail."

Groaning, she smacked her forehead. "I'm sorry. I forgot to charge it last night and plugged it in earlier before I pulled everything out of the garage. It's still sitting on the kitchen counter."

"No worries." He held up the bag. "I found you just in time for lunch if you're hungry. I stopped at a deli and got Italian heroes, soda, and chips."

Her stomach picked that moment to growl. "Actually, I'm starving. The last thing I ate was some oatmeal around seven this morning. When you pulled up, I'd been thinking about going inside to grab a couple of granola bars, but a hero sounds so much better. Thank you."

"My pleasure."

"Can you watch my money till for a minute?" She pointed at the old cigar box she was using. They'd found it in her aunt's bedroom filled with costume jewelry. "I need to use the bathroom. I have most of the cash on me, so there's only about twenty dollars in change in there."

"Sure. If anyone wants to buy something, I'll tell them to wait for you."

She waved her hand. "Most of the stuff has price tags, and I've been letting people haggle. I want to get rid of as much of it as possible. Whatever they offer that sounds reasonable, take it. I'll grab some napkins, cups with ice, and my damn phone. Do we need anything else?"

"Nope. In fact, we don't need the napkins. There are some in the bag."

"Great. I'll be right back."

Allie hurried inside, used the bathroom, then quickly double-checked the entire house to ensure no pictures of her and nothing with her real name on it was in view. Relieved nothing would give away her secret, she hid a large portion of the cash in a kitchen cabinet, grabbed her phone from the counter, filled two red plastic cups with ice, and brought them back outside.

West had found another lawn chair and put it next to hers, then added an empty box between them as a makeshift dining table. The soda bottles and still-wrapped food were on top of it as he waited for her to return. Her stomach growled as if thrilled it would be getting something more substantial than granola.

While eating, they were interrupted several times by people wanting to buy something, and each time Allie got up from her chair, West followed suit. He helped out when he could while swatting away the occasional bees and flies from their food until they could finish it.

As the afternoon progressed, Allie sold more than she'd expected to—close to eight hundred dollars' worth of items. West made some sales while she'd been busy with other customers and had carried bulky or heavy things to a few people's vehicles. By the time four-thirty rolled around, Allie had very little left to put back into the garage. Mrs. Marcus and Mrs. Kim had done well, too, and West helped them return their remaining things to their homes.

It was a little after five when everything was

cleaned up, and Allie invited West inside. "There's not much to eat here, and I'm too tired to go out, but we can order a pizza. I have a six-pack of Budweiser and some wine in the fridge." At home, she wasn't a big drinker but liked to have an occasional beer or a glass of chardonnay with her dinners.

"Sounds good."

"I need to shower first." After everything she'd done that day, she was sweaty, dusty, and dirty.

West leered at her. "That sounds even better. Want some company?"

Instead of giving him a verbal reply, she started stripping as she walked backward toward the bathroom with a come-hither stare. West kicked off his sneakers and followed her, removing his own clothing as he stalked closer. When he picked up his pace, she squealed and dashed down the hall with him hot on her heels. She only got one foot on the bathroom tile before he caught her around the waist, spun her around, and pressed her against the counter, ravaging her mouth with his own. As much as she wanted to wash away the day's dirt and grime, she wanted West even more.

Reaching into the shower, he blindly fumbled around until he found the handle and turned the water on to warm up.

As it always seemed to do when his hands and

mouth were on her, Allie's brain shut down. Hunger for the man took over her entire body. Her pulse increased, sending molten lava through her veins. His cock was long and stiff between them, with sticky pre-cum leaking from the tip onto her abdomen. The hair on his chest raked her hypersensitive nipples, sending jolts of electricity straight to her clit. Her pussy wept.

She roamed her hands over every ridge and valley of his hard flesh as his lips teased their way up her jawline. A shiver skated down her back as his hot breath tickled her ear. "Damn, woman, I can't get enough of you."

She knew exactly how he felt but couldn't think of any response. He nuzzled her neck, and she tilted her head to the side to give him better access. The two vanity mirrors were fogged over, and it was impossible to know if it was from the steam coming from the shower or the carnal heat emanating from skin-on-skin contact.

West tested the running water with his hand. "Perfect. Get in."

He helped her into the tub and then joined her. After closing the glass door, he urged her under the spray, and she tipped her head back to drench her hair, moaning as the hot water sluiced down onto her shoulders and below.

Picking up her shampoo bottle, he poured some of

the honeydew-scented liquid into his hand. "Turn around."

When she complied, he lathered her auburn strands and massaged her scalp. She'd never had a man wash her hair before, and the act was more erotic than she'd ever thought it could be. Her eyelids fell as she leaned back against his chest. "Mmm. That feels so good."

After he rinsed her hair, he grabbed her shower puff and bodywash and cleaned her from head to toe, dropping to his knees and giving her breasts, ass, and pussy extra attention. When he was done, she stepped back under the spray to flush away the suds. Still kneeling, West sucked her tits and lightly abraded her clit with the loofah. The stimulating combination was exhilarating, making her delirious with lust and need. Moments later, Allie was shocked when she came with little warning, slapping her hands against the wet tiles as her legs shook and she yelled his name. West wrapped his arms around her hips to steady her. "You're gorgeous when you come. Fucking gorgeous."

She panted and sagged against the shower wall as he stood again. While she recovered, he washed his hair, but when he picked the loofah up, she took it from him with a smirk. "Let me return the favor."

Heat flared in his eyes. "Be my guest."

She lathered the loofah and then rasped it over

every inch of his skin, except his cock and balls. He hissed then moaned every time she came close before skirting around them. "Little tease."

A giggle escaped her. "And you're enjoying every minute of it."

"Hell, yeah."

Instead of using the natural sponge, she soaped up her hands, gently cupped his balls with one, and grasped his shaft with the other. West gasped, and his head thudded against the wall. "Yes!"

She rolled his testicles as she tightened her grip on his cock. Her hand slid down, up, and twisted over the tip before repeating the process again. His hips rocked. She worked him harder and faster, studying his face for reactions. His teeth gnashed his bottom lip. His long eyelashes almost touched his cheeks, but she could feel his heated gaze on her.

He covered her hand with his, and his cock fucked their combined grip. Gripping her hair, he let out a deep growl. "Suck the tip."

Leaning forward, she swiped her tongue over the reddish-purple head, lapping up a pearly drop seeping from the slit. She parted her lips just enough to draw him into her mouth and then hollowed her cheeks.

"Oh, fuck, yeah! Allie!"

She did it again, bobbing her head slightly since their hands prevented her from taking more of him. He cursed again as his body seized, and hot, salty cum shot from him in streams, coating their hands and her face, neck, and breasts. It was dirty and raunchy, and she loved every bit of it.

As she'd done earlier, he collapsed against the wall. Gulping for air, he petted her head and then helped her stand. Without letting her rinse off his cum, he bent down and took possession of her mouth, letting their tongues tango. She'd never been with a man who wanted to taste himself on her, and realizing he was enjoying it was titillating.

They spent a few minutes basking in the aftermath of their climaxes, kissing, and cleaning up again. She could've stayed in there for another hour, making love to West, but eventually, the water cooled, and they had to get out. As they were drying themselves off with green, fluffy towels, West froze, and then his head fell backward as he groaned. "Shit."

"What?"

"I have to put my dirty clothes back on to run out to the truck. I hoped you'd invite me to stay, so I packed a duffel bag but left it on the passenger seat."

Allie giggled. "You could go out there in the towel, or I'm sure some of the neighbors wouldn't mind seeing you streak."

He burst out laughing. "Yeah, that's not gonna

happen. Neither is me going out in a towel. Get dressed and order the pizza while I get my bag."

"I can run outside and get it for you after I put some clothes on."

"Nope. I've got it. You just take care of the pizza. I'm starving. You wore me out, woman."

"Okay." Wrapping a towel around her body, she followed him into the hallway and shook her head as he pulled on his jeans, sans underwear, and his shirt. He didn't bother wearing his sneakers before heading toward the front door. Allie entered the spare bedroom, where she put on fresh underwear, yoga pants, and a David Bowie "Rebel Rebel" T-shirt. She didn't bother with a bra.

Forty minutes later, they sat on the couch, eating a Buffalo chicken pizza while watching reruns of *Cheers* on the TV. Apparently, West was a fan too. He was now dressed in black sweatpants and a blue tee. As he enjoyed a beer, Allie sipped a glass of wine. The scene was so domestic, like all the other times they'd eaten at his apartment, and it hurt knowing this would be their last Saturday night together.

Pushing the thought from her mind, she tried to savor what little time they had left.

After they cleaned up from dinner, West sat on the couch again and pulled her onto his lap. Lightly pinching her chin with his thumb and forefinger, he drew her closer for a kiss. It started sweet but soon became erotic, as if they hadn't had sex in days instead of only two hours ago.

Shifting, Allie straddled his hips and pressed her mound against his stiff cock, gasping into his mouth as lust combined with arousal and need. He pulled her shirt off and latched onto one breast. As she ran her fingers through his hair, his hands clutched her hips and aided her in riding him harder.

An orgasm built deep within her core, faster than she'd ever experienced, and when West bit her nipple, she couldn't stop the whirlwind that engulfed her if she tried. Her toes curled, and her back arched as colorful bokeh lights flashed behind her closed eyelids. "Ahhhh! My God! West! Yeeesssss! Yes!"

It was like being on a roller coaster, with vertical drops and dramatic three-hundred-sixty-degree loops. Her mind spun out of control, and she had no idea which way was up or down. The only thing grounding her was West's arms wrapped around her torso.

Finally, flushed and sated, Allie collapsed against West, trying desperately to replenish the oxygen her lungs craved. He let her rest briefly while nuzzling her neck. "Ready for more?"

"I don't know if I'll survive, but I'm willing to give it a go."

Chuckling, he pushed her to her feet and dragged

her yoga pants and underwear down. Using his broad shoulders for support, she stepped out of them. Instead of removing his sweatpants, he lifted his hips and pushed the material down to his knees. His majestic cock stood at attention, making her mouth water. His wallet was on one of the makeshift end tables, and he retrieved a condom from it. As he put it on, he said, "Turn around and put your feet on the outside of mine."

Oh, she liked where he was going with this. The reverse cowgirl position was one of her favorites, and it'd been a long time since she'd done it.

"Sit down, baby."

She nearly melted and wasn't sure if it was because of the growled order or the endearment. Either way, it weakened her knees until she obeyed his command without conscious thought. She settled on his lap with her legs spread, resting on the outside of his knees. His long, thick cock extended out from the apex of her thighs, its length flush against her labia. She lifted and tilted her pelvis until there was room for her to align the tip up with her slit. Her cunt was soaked and ready for him. Slowly, she eased down onto him, her body stretching to accommodate his girth. West groaned and muttered curses as her pussy enveloped him.

As she worked him deeper, he held onto her waist. "Fuck! You're so tight, I won't last long."

Her head fell back onto his shoulder as her breathing and heart rate increased. Slick sweat glazed their skin. Reaching around, he plucked and strummed one of her nipples while his other hand went south to her clit to torture the little bud. He bucked his hips, and she gyrated and fucked herself with his cock. They rutted like wild animals in heat. With every minute that passed, she climbed higher and higher toward the edge of euphoria, taking him with her.

"P-please, West . . . I need . . . oh my God . . . please!"

When she scratched the inside of his thigh while fondling his balls, he nipped her shoulder. "Damn, woman, what you do to me!"

Taking the lead, he tightened his grip on her hips and pummeled into her from below while her fingers replaced his on the little nub on her mound, massaging it. Their cries of pleasure grew louder, and the walls of her vagina spasmed with her impending climax. When the vortex peaked, it threw her over the edge, screaming as she tumbled into space. Moments later, he howled and stiffened beneath her, following her into oblivion.

She gasped for air and leaned back against him as his chest heaved.

"Holy shit. That—that . . . was . . ." Words to

describe what she'd just experienced wouldn't formulate in her mind, and she sighed.

West chuckled, and her breasts jiggled with the movement. "Yup, I agree. That . . . that was . . ."

An unladylike snort escaped her when he didn't complete the sentence. God, she was going to miss him. Thankfully, she was too blissed out for heartache to overtake her.

Chapter 12

After discarding the condom in the bathroom, West joined her in the spare bedroom, where she was already under the covers, totally spent from their lovemaking. He pointed to the other side of the queen-sized mattress and said, "Roll onto your side."

As she complied, he climbed under the covers and spooned her from behind. They rested in silence for a few minutes, basking in the afterglow, before he asked, "Have you ever been in love?"

"No." The lie came out too quickly, and she tried to shrug it off. "I thought I might have been a few times, but true love is supposed to hurt when it's gone, right?"

"That's always been my belief. You never really

heal when you honestly love someone and they die or move on without you."

Or they betray you.

She pushed the distasteful thought from her mind. Over the past few weeks, he'd proven time and again he was no longer the immature boy he'd been in tenth grade. He'd grown so much, and not only physically. She'd fallen for him harder this time than when she'd been a teenager. Back then, it'd been puppy love—a desire to be his that she'd doubted would ever happen. But now, when she left for Denver, she would be leaving her heart behind along with what might've been had she been honest with him from the start. What they shared now had helped heal the hurt she'd endured for the past twenty years. She was certain if their budding relationship had a chance to develop into something more, time would completely erase the "incident" from her mind.

"What about you? Have you ever been in love?"

"Once."

Surprised by his admission, she flipped over and curled into his chest. "Tell me."

He snorted. "You really want to hear about how my heart was crushed."

"If you don't want to tell me, that's okay, but I'm interested in who was stupid enough to walk away from you." Like she would be doing soon.

Running a hand over the smooth skin of her hip, he let out a sigh. "You'll probably think it's silly, but it was in high school." When Allie unexpectedly froze, West chuckled, not knowing what she was thinking. "Yup, you heard me—high school. In my sophomore year, there was a girl I really liked. She wasn't like most of the girls in our class—you know, the ones who were popular and stuck up and only wanted to date the guys who were popular too. Mostly jocks, like I was. As a quarterback on the junior varsity and varsity teams, I had girls hanging all over me and asking me out on dates—not that I minded, of course. After all, I was a horny teenager. But this one girl was really shy but super smart, and smart women have always turned me on—that's why I found you so attractive the first night we met. I mean, you're gorgeous, too, but it was your intelligence and wit that I couldn't get enough of. Still can't."

He shifted until she was tucked into the crook of his shoulder and then slowly stroked her bare back. "Anyway, something about this girl drew me in like a moth to a flame, so I pretended I didn't understand chemistry and asked her to tutor me. She tutored a few of us for months, but I never got the courage to ask her out when everyone else was around, and she would be the first one out of the library after our sessions. When it was almost the end of the school year, I had to give it a shot. Otherwise, I'd regret it all summer."

Oh, no, no, no, no. There's no way he's talking about you! This has to be a dream! Please don't let it be real!

Her prayer wasn't answered as he continued. "So, Allondra was at her locker . . ." She winced when he said her given name. ". . . and I walked right up and asked her to the Sophomore Social—that's an annual dance." Regret filled his voice. "I can still remember her response—*no, thanks*. Plain and simple, as if I'd asked if she needed a pen or something. Then, she practically ran away. I was crushed, completely heart-broken, and never went to the dance. I barely saw her for the rest of the school year—she stopped tutoring. Then I found out a few weeks after school ended that she moved out West somewhere, and I never saw her again."

Allie was stunned, her mind racing in every direc-tion at once. She couldn't believe it. This couldn't be happening. She'd gotten it wrong for twenty years, carrying the misplaced hurt and anger in her heart. All that time, she thought he'd asked her to humiliate her in front of the rest of the class. "That was real? I thought it was a cruel joke."

She didn't realize she'd said the words aloud, just a little more than a whisper until West stiffened against her. Allie was afraid to move. Afraid to face him or say anything more. Oh, God. If he figured out who she was . . .

But it was too late to take back the last fifteen seconds.

"What do you mean you—*you thought* it was a cruel joke? How did you know about . . ."

Fear shot through every cell in her body as she could almost hear his brain putting the puzzle pieces together.

"Holy shit!" Ripping off the covers, West leaped from the bed faster than a jackrabbit. Wide-eyed, she watched as he stood with his back to her, yanking on his discarded sweatpants. He stalked across the room, running his hands through his hair, making it stick up more than it had already been. When he finally turned around, the rage in his gaze was like needle pricks piercing her skin.

Setting his hands on his hips, he glared at her. "Y-you're not *Allie McKenna,* are you? You're *Allondra Dawson*, right? That's why I couldn't shake the feeling we'd met before, *right*? But you knew who I was, didn't you? *Didn't you?*" His voice grew harder and louder with every word he spoke. "You've been lying to me since day one! Haven't you?"

She couldn't respond as her eyes filled with tears, a lump took up residence in her throat, and her heart pounded with shock and horror. Although she always knew there was a chance he would find out who she really was sooner or later, nothing could've prepared her for his response—not that she blamed him one bit. Especially after discovering it was a huge misunderstanding in high school. She couldn't comprehend why those girls had said it was a joke, but it didn't matter now.

"What the hell is this, *Allondra?*" He moved closer and gestured between them. "You thought I was playing a joke on you in high school by asking you to the dance? *So, what the hell is this?*" he repeated. "A revenge *fuck* for something I didn't do? Tell me!"

Pushing up into a sitting position, she reached for him and cringed when he stepped further away again. "I-I'm sorry, West. I didn't know. I-I didn't mean for it to go this far. You're right. I . . . I recognized you that first night and . . . and everything I felt that day in high school came rushing back. I-I heard some girls talking in—in the bathroom a few days earlier about how you were going to embarrass me by inviting me to the dance and then standing me up! I-I didn't think you really meant it when you asked me out, I swear!"

The tears rolled down her cheeks like a floodgate had opened, and she couldn't wipe them away fast enough. As she tried to explain, he found his shirt and pulled it on before shoving his feet into his sneakers without bothering to put on his socks.

"I don't fucking believe this!" He ran his hands down his face, which was red with fury. The veins in his temples throbbed to the point Allie could see them. "So, the whole time we were together, you what? You were getting your kicks, thinking you were getting even for something that wasn't true? And on top of everything, I just confessed that I was in love with you back then and you broke my heart. Going through that the first time was hard enough, but now I have to deal with it again. That's got to be the icing on your cake, right?" West didn't wait for a response as he grabbed his keys, phone, and wallet from the nightstand. His tone grew deathly low. "You know what? Never mind. You did it. You got your retribution, Allondra. I hope you're happy."

"W-West, I'm s-sorry! I didn't mean—"

Her apology was cut off as he stormed out of the bedroom, slamming the door shut behind him. Anguish bloomed in her chest, so painful she might've thought it was a heart attack if she didn't know it was splitting in two from grief. A moment later, the front door also closed with a bang. Allie cried harder when West's truck engine roared to life and its tires screeched as he peeled out onto the street.

Chapter 13

A horn blared behind Allie's car, jolting her from her woolgathering. Focusing on the road, she accelerated and drove through the light that'd turned green at some point. Four weeks had passed since West figured out who she was and three since she returned to Denver. Today was another day of zoning out at the most inappropriate moments, recalling her time with him from when she'd walked into his pub until he'd walked out of her life and everything in between. She could replay every second of their lovemaking as if they were episodes of a favorite TV show. But then the memories all ended the same—with the fury in his eyes, the confusion then anger and agony in his voice, and finally, the slamming of the door.

She'd wanted to go to him and apologize again and again until he forgave her, but it wouldn't do any good.

The damage was done, and there was no going back. She'd driven past the pub several times but never stopped, not wanting to cause a scene at his place of business or the apartment house he owned. That would've pushed in the hypothetical knife she'd stabbed him with even further. She'd already hurt him enough—the best thing for West was for her to leave him alone.

Unfortunately, Allie couldn't figure out what was best for her. She needed to move forward—to forget the last seven weeks ever happened—but it was easier said than done. Her co-workers had noticed her misery. Apparently, she'd been moping around the office, distracted to the point some people had needed to snap their fingers in front of her face or touch her to get her attention. Today, she'd been called into her boss's office for a "chat." The woman had asked if she wanted to speak to one of the counselors on staff to work through whatever was bothering her. Everyone thought she was still grieving her aunt's death, and Allie continued to let them believe that. Announcing what had really happened to cause her sorrow would be far too embarrassing.

What had started as sweet revenge had ended with her falling in love with the man who now hated her.

As usual, Sadie had been her sounding board over the last few weeks, but it was time to let the subject die. Her cousin had to be tired of talking about West and listening to Allie cry over him. Somehow, she'd been able to put on a convincing smile and a happy tone in her voice whenever she saw her mom because the older woman hadn't suspected anything was wrong. They planned to have dinner the next night, and Allie would tell her mother that she wanted to stay in Denver. If things had ended differently with West, she would've already put in for a transfer and been packing up her condo. But there was no way she could ever face him again. It was painful enough to think of him.

Trying to put West out of her mind, at least until she was parked and unable to cause an accident, she focused on the traffic and what to have for dinner. For some stupid reason, she was craving a grilled cheese sandwich, and that brought back the memory of the first time she was at the Cat & Fiddle. The night she'd eaten the best damn grilled cheese of her life, realized the man behind the bar was West Lockhart, and slept with him.

Great, now her head was filled with thoughts of him again. Damn it.

Pulling into her complex's lot, she parked in her assigned space and turned off the engine. Before she opened the door, though, something by the building's side entrance caught her attention. No, not something, but someone. And not just anyone, but West! She had to be hallucinating.

He was exactly how she remembered, as handsome as ever and sculpted to perfection. She recognized him even with sunglasses shielding his eyes and what appeared to be a two-day beard and mustache, which brought to mind how those coarse whiskers rasped over her nipples and inner thighs. She squeezed her legs together to tamp down the instant arousal those thoughts conjured up.

In a blue button-down shirt with the sleeves rolled up—fuck, she loved his arm porn—he leaned against the brick wall with his hands in the front pockets of his black dress pants, staring in her direction. It was as if he knew her car and that she was sitting in it. His expression was blank—what she could see of it—as he bided his time.

What was he doing here? How was he here? Due to her security clearance, Allie's personal information wasn't listed on any searchable websites.

Swallowing the sudden lump in her throat and keeping her gaze on him, afraid he would disappear if she glanced away, she felt around the passenger seat and grabbed her purse, briefcase, and phone. West didn't change position as she climbed out of the car, pushed the locked button, and shut the door. Despite his sunglasses, she could tell he was tracking her every movement. Praying she wouldn't trip over something and face-plant, Allie crossed the parking lot and trudged up the walkway, trepidation in her every step. He hadn't moved a muscle in all that time, and she stopped a few feet away from him, unable to say a solitary word.

Almost a full minute ticked by before he crossed his arms and spoke. "You should have a talk with your neighbors about safety around here." His familiar, deep, rumbling voice sent shivers down her spine. "The little old lady in three-ten was all too happy to tell me which parking spot was yours and that you always used this entrance."

"Wh-what are you—?" she sputtered. "H-how—?" Her mind couldn't fill in the blanks.

"What am I doing here, and how did I know where you lived?"

All Allie could do was nod as she continued to gawk at him.

West dropped his gaze to the ground and rubbed his index finger over his chin. "Well, your cousin Sadie came to visit me last week. Now I know where you took the last name McKenna from. By the way, she's a force to be reckoned with. Anyway, she sat me down and explained everything that happened back in high school—everything you tried to explain that day, but I was too pissed to listen to. She also told me how much you regretted sleeping with me under false pretenses that first night."

Taking off his sunglasses, he hung them from the V of his shirt, created by the undone top two buttons. Unexplained remorse flashed in his blue eyes as he studied her. "Allondra—"

"Allie, please," she managed to croak out. Her legs were shaking, but somehow, she was still standing. "No —no one calls me Allondra anymore except my mom and aunts and uncles."

"Okay. I had no idea you were the target of the mean girls in high school, Allie. If I had, I would've put a stop to it. I finally remembered that I told my friend Ryan that I was going to ask you to the dance." He shrugged. "I guess he told a few others, and it got around. I swear I didn't know people were saying I was only doing it to be cruel and that I would stand you up. I really, *really* wanted to go with you. That's the God's honest truth."

Hot tears rolled down her cheeks, and when the door beside West opened from the inside, she turned her face away, not wanting one of her neighbors to see her crying. She swiped her eyes as footsteps headed toward the parking lot.

Once she was certain they were alone, Allie faced West again. "I believe you. I just wish I knew that back then." She sniffled, and her gaze darted around as she tried to find the courage to say her next words. "I still owe you a huge apology."

"Yeah." He bit his lip and nodded for a moment. "Yeah, you do. And I'm willing to listen to it this time."

Oh, thank God. She still didn't understand why he was here and what would happen after she groveled and begged for forgiveness, but at least he would let her do that. She swallowed hard. "Th-thank you. Can we . . . do you mind if we go upstairs to my condo? I'd rather not talk out here where anyone can walk up and hear us."

Taking a step to the side, he gestured to the door. "After you."

After briefly fumbling around in her purse, Allie found her keys with the fob needed to release the door lock. When it clicked, West reached over and held the door open for her. Once inside, he offered to carry her briefcase, and she numbly handed it over. He followed her down the hallway to the elevator, and they silently rode up to the fifth floor. Moments later, they were in her condo.

As she deposited her keys, phone, and purse on the kitchen counter, West set her briefcase on one of the dining room chairs as he passed it before striding into the living room. "Nice. Your setup is similar to mine, but you have a much better view."

His apartment overlooked busy Bartlett Avenue in

Holden, while Allie's unit had a gorgeous view of a large lake and park across the street from the building.

She kicked off her pumps and removed a pair of sheer Peds and then the navy-blue suit jacket that went with her dress pants. A white sleeveless top and understated jewelry completed the outfit.

Trying to give herself another few moments to gather her thoughts, she asked, "Can I get you something to drink? Water? Soda? I have some Coors or wine too."

"A beer would be good, thanks."

Allie was grateful for his choice because she could use a little alcohol to calm her nerves. Grabbing two cold bottles from the fridge, she popped the tops off, took a deep breath, then carried them into the living room, handing him one. After they both took several gulps, she gestured for him to sit on the couch. Wanting to keep some distance between them, she sat at the other end, tucking one foot underneath her. Being any closer to him would mess with her concentration. He wouldn't be there if she didn't have a chance to set things right, and she doubted she would get another one if she screwed it up.

She sighed heavily and picked at the beer label with her fingernail. "Please let me talk without interrupting. Otherwise, I'll never get through it. I didn't think I'd see you again—to have a chance to apologize—

but that didn't stop me from practicing in my head what I would say to you over these past four weeks."

When he nodded and indicated with a flash of his hand for her to continue, she licked her lips. "I'm sorry, West, so very sorry. I know that doesn't mean much right now, but . . ." Dropping her gaze to the couch, she found it easier to talk when she couldn't see him. "I'm sure Sadie explained what she could, but you should hear it all from me. I liked you a lot back in high school. I mean, I was totally crushing on you, but I never thought I'd be someone you were attracted to. You were the hottest guy in school, popular, sweet, and funny. You didn't horse around like the others did when I tried to tutor them. Instead, I knew you were really listening to me. I was thrilled when I thought you were passing Chemistry because of me. It was a boost to my fragile ego back then. But I was the shy, geeky girl with braces, glasses, and too many curves in all the wrong places. I couldn't imagine you liking me beyond maybe a friend.

"When I overheard those girls joking about how you were going to ask me to the dance and then stand me up, I believed them. I was hiding in one of the restroom stalls, so they didn't know I was there, and when they left, I stayed and cried through the next period." Her eyes welled up at the memory, and she snatched a tissue from a box on the long table behind the couch. They were always handy for when she watched a tearjerker on Netflix.

After wiping her eyes, she forged ahead. "I was so insecure back then, and the thought of you, my crush, doing that to me was so painful. I don't know how I managed not to bawl in front of you and everyone else when you asked me to the dance, but somehow, I did. And then, like you said, I ran away. I was so depressed that summer between you and moving to Denver. But then I made friends here, grew up some more, and blossomed in college. I never forgot how angry I was at you, though. I hurt for twenty years over that experience and had no idea it might have ended differently if I hadn't heard those girls and said yes to you."

She took a few swigs from her beer and noticed it was nearly empty. She was shocked when West stood, took the bottle from her, strode into the kitchen, and retrieved two more. Apparently, he'd finished his too. When he returned, he handed her one of the bottles and retook his seat, remaining silent.

Allie inhaled and blew out a fast breath. This next part would be more difficult to get through. "When I saw you that first night at the pub, all that anger and hurt came rushing to the forefront of my mind again. To me, you were the cause of all my mental anguish back then. It's not fair to pin it on you, especially with what I know now, but that's what being a teenager does to you. You're so impressionable at that age and not mature enough to think things through.

"I swear, I've never done anything like I did to you in my life, but something evil took over my mind that night. At first, I wanted to get the hell out of there. Then I wanted to scream and yell at you. But when I realized you didn't recognize me at all, I saw a chance to get revenge for what I thought you did to me. It was wrong. I knew it that night, and by the next morning, I regretted everything. No matter what, you didn't deserve to be used like that. I was never a cocktease or a slut, or someone who actually exacted revenge on anyone else. Yeah, I'd thought about it before, in general. Everyone wishes karma would get those who earned it, but I never dished it out.

"I was miserable when I left your apartment in the middle of the night. You were so nice and interesting, and I had sex with you out of spite. It was so unlike me, and I hated myself for doing it. I barely slept for days until we ran into each other at the Home Depot. I thought Fate was fucking with me. I mean, what are the chances we'd both be in the paint department at the same time that early on a Friday morning?"

She closed her eyes and breathed deeply, trying to get her emotions under control. Her chin quivered, and more tears fell, but she forced herself to finish what she'd started.

"The more we saw each other, the more my hurt and humiliation were pushed away while other feelings replaced them. I started falling for you the night we went to your friends' restaurant. I saw you as someone completely different and not the boy who tried to embarrass me in front of our entire school, which you obviously didn't do. You were the guy I always wanted to fall in love with—sweet, funny, intelligent, caring, and much more. And I did fall in love with you, but it was too late to confess who I really was. I was selfish, though, and wanted to save as many new memories of you as possible to comfort myself when I came home and was lonely again. To erase what I thought you'd done to me."

She wiped her wet cheeks again and finally met his gaze. She couldn't tell what he was thinking because of the blank expression on his face, and her gut twisted. "I'm sorry, West. I don't deserve your forgiveness—hell, I don't deserve to be in the same room with you—but I'm asking you to please forgive me, even if you never want to see me again."

Silence filled the room for several moments before he asked, "Is that it?"

Allie reeled back as if he'd slapped her. His eyes widened in alarm, and he grabbed her free hand. "No, no, no, no, no! That's not what I meant! I'm sorry, Allie. You asked me to wait until you were done talking, and I've been over here, biting my tongue to keep from interrupting you. I just wanted to know if I could speak now."

Her shoulders sagged, and she nodded. "Yes, you can."

He scooted closer to her. "First of all, those glasses and curves you thought were in the wrong places were part of my attraction back then. Yeah, the braces might've been an issue—no guy wants to imagine metal in a girl's mouth when he's dreaming of her giving him a blowjob. But those weren't permanent. Everything else you had going on was pretty hot. I told you intelligence has always been a huge draw for me—every time you answered a question correctly in class, I was in awe.

"But I can't imagine what you were going through in high school when you thought I was about to play a vile joke on you. And I'll admit I was pissed and hurt when I realized who you were a few weeks ago—there's no denying that. But as the days passed, my anger faded, but the pain grew stronger. I finally realized I was hurting so much because I'd fallen in love with you too. I tried to tell myself that you weren't worth the torture I was going through, but that was a lie. Remember when I said it's true love when you never heal when the other person dies or moves on without you?"

"Yes," she whispered.

"I always thought true insta-love happened to other people or in books and movies. I never thought it would happen to me. But I was right—my heart wouldn't heal after you were gone. You've been on my mind since I left your aunt's house. I knew you would always be the one who got away if I didn't do something. I went through a broad range of emotions over the past four weeks, finally identifying it and putting a name to all of it. Grief. I was going through the seven stages of grief. The final one is acceptance and hope, and that's why I'm here, Allie. I forgive you. I love you. I don't want to live without you. And I hope you feel the same."

Her teardrops became two rivers running down her face. She lunged forward and threw her arms around him, sobbing into his neck. His beard abraded her temple. She wasn't worthy of him or his forgiveness, but there he was, saying he loved and wanted her in his life.

His hands gently gripped both sides of her head and lifted. Their gazes met, and she saw the truth in his. He wasn't fucking with her and getting his own retribution for what she'd done to him. There was desire, love, and her future in his eyes.

Chapter 14

Leaning down, West pressed his mouth to hers. When her lips parted for him, his fingers threaded into her hair and gripped the strands, holding her in place. He pulled back only an inch or two, his gaze scanning her face. Everything he experienced, he saw reflected back to him. Love, desire, want, and need.

His hand tightened in her hair as he slammed his mouth down on hers and tried not to lose his barely-there control. He didn't want sex tonight—he wanted to make love to her. This was the woman who'd been made for him. If he had his way, she'd be moving back to Holden, or he'd be picking up his roots and laying them down again in Denver. Either way, his future was with Allie—it was carved into his heart.

Pulling on her hair, he exposed and feasted on her

neck—nibbling, sucking, and licking every inch he could reach. She moaned as she pulled her shirt out of her waistband. Unable to wait for her to remove it, he pushed the hem up, exposing a nude-colored bra. He yanked down one of the cups and played with the distended rosy peak he found. Allie cried out and struggled to remove her clothes.

It seemed like eons since she'd been in his arms, but she was as responsive as ever. He would never get enough of this woman. Fifty years from now, he would still want her—need her.

"W-West . . . b-bed . . . more room."

While he hated to stop if only for a brief moment, a big mattress where they could spread out sounded inviting. Getting to his feet, he helped her stand, then followed her as she led him into the bedroom. They peeled off their clothes, their hungry gazes never leaving the other's body.

Once naked, Allie crawled onto the bed and beckoned West to join her. There was no way in hell he would turn her down, but he needed a moment to ward off his impending orgasm for a little bit longer.

His heart pounded in his chest and resonated in his ears as he stared down at her with his hand wrapped around his rock-hard shaft. He licked his lips in anticipation. "You're beautiful, baby. So damn beautiful." His voice was gruff and filled with lust.

Maybe making slow love would have to wait for the second time. He needed to be inside her soon, fucking her like a madman, but he had to prepare her first.

An adorable blush spread across her chest and face, revving his engine even more. He'd only had one beer and a few sips of the second one, but he was drunk on her once more—Allie was more intoxicating than any woman he'd ever known.

Climbing onto the bed next to her, he stopped beside her legs and leaned down to nip one hipbone and then the other before his gaze found her face again. Pushing against her inner thighs, West spread her wide. Her pussy glistened, and her folds were nicely swollen. He ran the back of his forefinger over them, causing her to squirm.

"Please, West!"

"Mmm. I'll never tire of you begging for my cock." Bending down, he rasped his tongue up her slit, reveling in her taste. She bucked her pelvis and pleaded for him to do it again.

He draped his arm over her hips, trapping and holding them in place as he gave her sweet, bare pussy his full attention. His cock throbbed against the mattress. Tucking his hands under her ass cheeks, he squeezed them before lifting her to give himself better access. He stiffened his tongue and tunneled inside her, making her gasp and grab a handful of his hair. "Oh! West! More! Oh, please!"

After eating her out for a few minutes, he moved upward and found her exposed clit. He teased the little pearl, flicking his tongue over it before sucking on it hard. He released her ass so he could use his fingers to fuck her until she came for him. He eased one and then two of them into her drenched core. Her hips undulated as he drove her higher and higher. Her moans became louder. West's cock threatened to explode from the sounds of Allie chasing her orgasm. She was killing him.

He curled his fingers and found her G-spot, rubbing it as he lapped at her clit. Knowing he wouldn't last long once he was inside her, he wanted her to fly for him. Reaching up with his other hand, he tweaked her nipple. She clutched the bedspread with both hands, twisting it as a wail of pleasure erupted from her lungs.

The walls of her cunt quivered, then clenched around his fingers, almost crushing them. She bucked her hips, and her legs shook as the climax claimed her. Using his hands and mouth, West drew out her release as long as possible until it ebbed.

While she gulped for air, Allie's sated, flushed body sagged against the mattress. West removed his fingers and deliberately licked them slowly, one by one.

Through heavy eyelids, she watched him as a sexy smile spread across her face. "Your tongue is very talented."

He grinned at the compliment. "Only for you, baby. From now on, my tongue will never touch another woman."

Her own tongue peeked out and licked her lips, causing him to groan as he crawled up her body. He cupped her breast and laved the nipple before giving the other one the same attention.

When he couldn't wait anymore, West pushed up to find his pants and the condom in his wallet, but Allie grasped his arm and stopped him. "I'm clean and on the pill."

Dazed, he gaped at her. "I'm clean too. I had an annual physical right before we met. Are you sure?"

"Yes. I want you with nothing between us."

Fuck, he wanted that more than anything else in the world. He'd never gone bareback with a woman before, and right then, he was thankful for the fact. Allie would be his first. His only.

He covered her body with his own and leaned on his forearms, keeping most of his weight off her. Pumping his hips, he rubbed his cock over her sensitive clit. She panted and writhed beneath him. "Now, West! Please!"

Clenching his jaw, he eased his swollen red crown

inside her as she wrapped her legs around his hips. His eyes slammed shut, and his body tensed with restraint. "Shit! You're so fucking tight. So hot and wet."

Her passage was like an inferno, burning him alive. Nothing could've prepared him for the sensations that assailed him without a latex barrier between them. He would never buy another box of the damn things.

She dug her heels into his ass, urging him on. "Don't hold back."

"I don't think I could if I tried."

A few more thrusts and he was balls deep inside her. When she clenched around him, he tensed. "Hang on a second, baby. Otherwise, I won't last long enough to make you come again."

While her pelvis stilled, her nails scratched across his back. Damn, how he'd missed her doing that.

After regaining some semblance of control, he retreated and then plunged back in, setting a slow pace that soon picked up speed. The headboard banged against the wall with every thrust of his hips. He nuzzled her neck before plundering her mouth again. Their tongues tangled together. A tingling started in his spine, and his balls drew up into his scrotum. He shifted to change the angle of his pelvis, then fucked her harder and faster. Moments later, her second orgasm crested, and he surrendered to his own.

Throwing his head back, West ejaculated inside her with a growling roar.

A little while later, after he'd cleaned them both up with a wet towel, Allie cuddled against his chest. Slaked and sleepy, she yawned and rested her leg on top of his thighs. "I never thought I'd see you again, much less be with you again."

He brushed his lips across the top of her head. "You'll never have to worry about that again. You own me, sweet baby—mind, body, heart, and soul."

"You own me too. I love you."

"I love you, Allie. I never stopped. We may have taken the long road to get here, but from now on, I want to walk with you by my side for the rest of my life if you'll let me."

Then she said the word he'd waited twenty years to hear. "Yes."

Other Books by Samantha Cole

**Denotes titles/series that are only available on select digital sites. Paperbacks and audiobooks are available on most book sites.

TRIDENT SECURITY SERIES

Leather & Lace

His Angel

Waiting For Him

Not Negotiable: A Novella

Topping The Alpha

Watching From the Shadows

Whiskey Tribute: A Novella

Tickle His Fancy

No Way in Hell: A Steel Corp/Trident Security Crossover (co-authored with J.B. Havens)

Absolving His Sins

Option Number Three: A Novella

Salvaging His Soul

Trident Security Field Manual

Torn In Half: A Novella

Master Cordell

HAZARD FALLS SERIES

Don't Fight It

Don't Shoot the Messenger

COCK & BULL SERIES

Scout

Rico

MALONE BROTHERS SERIES

Her Secret

Her Sleuth

LARGO RIDGE SERIES

Cold Feet

ANTELOPE ROCK SERIES

(CO-AUTHORED WITH J.B. HAVENS)

Wannabe in Wyoming

Wistful in Wyoming

AWARD-WINNING STANDALONE BOOKS

The Road to Solace

Scattered Moments in Time: A Collection of Short Stories &
More

Standalone Books

Sweet Revenge (A Novella)

The Sugarplum Fairy (A Novella)

***THE BID ON LOVE SERIES

(WITH 7 OTHER AUTHORS!)

Going, Going, Gone: Book 2

***THE COLLECTIVE: SEASON TWO

(WITH 7 OTHER AUTHORS!)

Angst: Book 7

***SPECIAL COLLECTIONS

Trident Security Series: Volume I

Trident Security Series: Volume II

Trident Security Series: Volume III

Trident Security Series: Volume IV

Trident Security Series: Volume V

Trident Security Series: Volume VI

About Samantha Cole

USA Today Bestselling Author and Award-Winning Author Samantha Cole is a retired policewoman and former paramedic. Using her life experiences and training, she strives to find the perfect mix of suspense and romance for her readers to enjoy.

Awards:

Wannabe in Wyoming (co-authored by J.B. Havens) won the bronze medal in the 2021 Readers' Favorite Awards in the General Romance category.

Scattered Moments in Time, won the gold medal in the 2020 Readers' Favorite Awards in the Fiction Anthology category.

The Road to Solace (formerly *The Friar*), won the silver medal in the 2017 Readers' Favorite Awards in the Contemporary Romance category.

Samantha has over thirty-five books published throughout several different series as well as a few standalone novels. A full list can be found on her website.

Sexy Six-Pack's Sirens Group on Facebook
Website: www.samanthacoleauthor.com
Newsletter: www.geni.us/SCNews

- facebook.com/SamanthaColeAuthor
- instagram.com/samanthacoleauthor
- bookbub.com/profile/samantha-a-cole
- goodreads.com/SamanthaCole
- amazon.com/Samantha-A-Cole/e/B00X53K3X8